The Boy Who Wished
The Man Who Received

Series: Forever His Destiny Series

Book : 1

By

Nathan Leigh Moffett

Table of Contents

Acknowledgement

I must offer my thanks to the Almighty God of the Bible, YAHWEH, who guided this entire journey. He provided the dreams, the visions, and the daily insights that shaped every page. This book is a testimony to His faithfulness—I am merely the pen in His hand.

To my Father & Mother

Thank you for life's memories, the lessons learned, and the guidance on how to live. Though you were taken from me before I could place this work in your hands, you shaped every part of who I became. Your love, your sacrifices, and the values you instilled continued to guide me long after you were gone. Even in your absence, you inspired me — steady as stars — and helped me finish a story I wish I could have shared with you both.

To anyone who has ever hidden who they are, to those who learned to whisper instead of speaking, to the ones who prayed to wake up different, this book is for you. May you find your voice. May you find your magic. May you one day stand in the light without fear.

To the dreamers, the ones who wished on stars, the ones who kept believing even when the world told them not to — you are the heartbeat of this story.

To the one I someday hope will walk beside me, thank you for living in my imagination before you ever walked into my life. This story was built from the dream of you — your strength, your gentleness, your loyalty, your fire, your hands, your heartbeat, your place beside mine. Wherever you are… I'll meet you when the time is right.

To every reader who found this book — thank you for letting me place my heart in your hands. May this story remind you that wishes don't have deadlines. That love doesn't expire. And that the universe remembers every prayer whispered by a lonely boy under the night sky.

With gratitude, hope, and starlight, *Nathan Leigh Moffett*

(1) A Wish I Never Outgrew

I've always been the kind of guy who wished on stars.

Yeah, even now, at twenty-five, with a steady job and a city apartment that feels like a fortress against my past. Some people grow out of it; I never did. When I was a kid, I believed that if you looked up at the right moment—just when the sky decided to pay attention—you could whisper something honest into the dark and maybe, just maybe, the universe would tuck it away for safekeeping. Those nights, lying on the dew-damp grass in our backyard, the stars felt like distant allies, winking back at my secrets while the crickets chirped a lullaby of indifference.

Back then, my wishes were simple, raw, and unspoken: Let me find someone who understands me. Someone gentle, someone strong. Someone who sees me without being told where to look. A companion who could match my quiet intensity, who wouldn't flinch at the parts of me I'd learned to hide.

I never said it aloud. You don't confess feelings like that when you grow up in a home where the Bible sits on the coffee table like a second parent, its leather cover worn from years of sermons and family devotions. My dad was a minister—full-time preacher with a voice that could thunder like judgment day, part-time businessman juggling real estate deals that kept the lights on. Somehow both jobs took all of him, leaving little room for questions that didn't have scripture-approved answers. Mom ran the house like she'd been born knowing the blueprints, her hands always busy with meals, laundry, or organizing church potlucks. And me? I was the last child of three... until my younger sibling showed up and shuffled the whole deck, turning me into the overlooked middle kid overnight. Suddenly, I was the bridge between the older siblings' achievements and the baby's innocent demands.

I wasn't unhappy. Not in the dramatic, storybook sense. We had laughter around the dinner table, holidays filled with hymns and homemade pies, and a sense of belonging that came from shared rituals. But I was careful. Vigilant, even. From the moment I was four years old, I knew something about me sparkled in a direction that wasn't allowed to shine. It was like carrying a lantern in a storm—beautiful, but dangerous if anyone noticed the flicker.

I remember being at the grocery store, clinging to Mom's skirt while she compared prices on canned peaches, when I saw a boy with sun-kissed skin and hair that glowed like it had swallowed the sunlight. He was maybe six, kicking his heels against the shopping cart while his mother chatted with the cashier. I stood there staring at him with the awe of a kid seeing magic for the first time—the way his freckles danced across his nose, the easy grin that lit up his face like a summer afternoon. My heart fluttered, a strange warmth blooming in my chest that had nothing to do with the store's fluorescent lights.

And I thought: That. Whatever that is… I like that. I want to be near that, to understand why it makes the world feel brighter.

But even then—even at four—I knew not to say a word. You hear things in conservative families, even if they're not aimed at you. Whispers about "getting help" for cousins who acted "different," stories about troubled teens disappearing into programs that promise to "fix" them with prayer circles and tough love, and rumors about kids who never made it back home, their families claiming they'd "found their way" elsewhere. The air in our town was thick with unspoken rules, enforced by Sunday sermons that painted love in narrow strokes—man and woman, Adam and Eve, no room for deviations.

So, I swallowed the truth down. Pressed it into the deepest part of me like a pressed flower hidden in a too-holy book, its petals preserved but never allowed to bloom. I buried it under layers of normalcy: helping Dad with yard work, memorizing Bible verses for youth group, and nodding along when friends talked about crushes on girls from school.

As I grew up, the world expected me to be predictable: church on Sundays, school with straight A's, manners that could charm the elderly ladies at potlucks, clean answers to every question.

And I did all that. I blended in seamlessly, like camouflage in a forest of expectations. I learned to laugh when people teased girls around me, even though I felt nothing but politeness—a polite detachment that masked the void inside. I dated a girl once in high school, a sweet church friend with braids and a laugh like bells, but our "relationship" was all hand-holding and awkward goodbyes, never igniting the spark I pretended to feel.

Inside was a different story. A turbulent sea of confusion and longing. I saw beauty in boys—manly, golden, confident boys with broad shoulders and easy smiles—and felt ashamed for reasons I didn't fully understand. Why me? Why this pull that felt as natural as breathing but as forbidden as theft? I prayed about it in the quiet of my room, knees pressed into the carpet, begging for change like it was a defect to be repaired. I cried about it once or twice, hot tears soaking my pillow as I wrestled with the fear of eternal damnation. But nothing changed. The feelings stayed. Quiet, loyal, persistent, like a heartbeat I couldn't silence.

I didn't touch another person—not the way I wanted to—for years. Not through the awkward teen years of locker room glances I forced myself to ignore, not during college where I buried myself in books and part-time jobs to avoid the temptation of dorm life. The isolation built walls around me, but it also sharpened my resolve—I wasn't going to risk everything for a fleeting moment.

Not until I was twenty-one. One night, trembling with a mix of fear and curiosity that made my hands shake on the steering wheel, I drove three hours to meet a guy from a website—a discreet corner of the internet where anonymity felt like armor. He was older, kind-eyed, with a voice that soothed my nerves over coffee where we explored feelings I'd never experienced. It was like waking from a long dream, colors flooding back into a grayscale world.

It was my first taste of truth. And my first new secret, one that felt like freedom laced with danger.

That moment lit a fire under me. Not a reckless one, the kind that burns everything down. A determined one, steady and purposeful, like a forge reshaping metal. I needed to know who I was outside the tight circles of small-town expectation, where every glance felt like scrutiny and every whisper carried judgment. I needed to grow without the constant feeling of being watched by God, neighbors, and family all at the same time— eyes that saw too much and understood too little. Though I felt this way, I also wanted to establish my own boundaries, the kind that would protect me and also allow me to be me.

So, I left. I packed up my little life—my faith (frayed but not abandoned), my fears (packed tightly like winter clothes), my hopes (fragile as glass ornaments), my old star-wish—and drove toward the city, half terrified of the unknown, half ready to claim it. The highway stretched like a promise, the radio playing songs of reinvention as rural fields gave way to urban sprawl.

The city swallowed me whole at first. Tall glass towers piercing the sky like ambitious fingers, endless movement of crowds pulsing through sidewalks, people rushing everywhere like they were late for destiny. Horns blared, lights flickered, and the air hummed with a thousand conversations I wasn't part of. But I liked it—the anonymity, the chaos that let me disappear and reemerge as someone new. A job came quickly—customer service for a giant tech company, answering calls in a cubicle farm that smelled of coffee and recycled air. Not glamorous, but stable. A chance to hide in plain sight. A chance to rebuild myself from the inside out, one cautious step at a time.

What I didn't know was that someone had already noticed me. Not in a creepy way, like shadows lurking in alleys. Not in a "stranger watching you through blinds" way, with malice or obsession. More like a quiet gravity, an invisible pull that drew orbits closer without announcement.

A presence that kept crossing paths with mine and then pretending it hadn't, like a game of cosmic hide-and-seek. Sometimes I'd walk into the building and feel like the air shifted, a subtle charge that raised the hairs on my arms. Sometimes I'd catch the silhouette of a man with dark bronze skin and a sharp profile in the distance—broad shoulders under a tailored shirt, moving as he belonged in every room he entered, his stride confident yet unhurried. I never had a reason to stare, so I didn't. I kept my head down, focused on scripts and screens, telling myself it was just the city's energy playing tricks.

But he stared enough for both of us. I didn't know that he paused when I laughed softly with coworkers during lunch breaks, my voice carrying a lightness I was just starting to reclaim. I didn't know he listened when I casually mentioned loving Disney movies during team-building icebreakers—the classics like *The Lion King*, with their themes of self-discovery that mirrored my own hidden journey. I didn't know I had sparked a curiosity in someone so self-contained that even his footsteps sounded disciplined, each one measured like a chess move.

I didn't know that he was already gathering details about me— not intrusively, like a stalker piecing together a puzzle from scraps, but deliberately, with the patience of a strategist studying a blueprint. An overheard comment here, a shared elevator glance there, building a mental map of who I might be beneath the polite exterior.

I didn't know that my simple hope—my old star-wish, whispered into countless nights—had finally begun to unfold behind the scenes, threads weaving together in ways I couldn't yet see.

I didn't know the man who would change everything for me… had already picked me out in a crowd, his interest blooming like a secret garden in the heart of the chaos.

But the universe did.

It always does, patient and precise, aligning the stars we once wished upon.

(2) The Man Behind Me in Line

The Starbucks in the heart of the city was predictably chaotic that morning, every table claimed, every chair occupied, and the line snaking from the counter nearly to the door as if the entire building's population had converged on the same caffeine altar at once. The air hung heavy with the rich, dark perfume of roasted beans, undercut by something sharper—burnt hope, perhaps, or the faint, metallic tang of corporate exhaustion that clung to everyone's clothes like secondhand smoke.

All I wanted was my drink: an Iced Peach Oolong Tea, the one bright, unapologetic choice in a menu otherwise dominated by bitter espresso and syrupy regret. I yawned, checked my watch, and adjusted the lanyard holding my still-new employee badge. I was new enough to arrive early out of diligence, hopeful enough to believe punctuality mattered, and tired enough to feel a low-grade irritation at the slow crawl of the queue.

That was when I felt it again—that subtle shift in the atmosphere, like the air itself had paused to take notice.

An awareness. Not paranoia, exactly, but the unmistakable sensation of someone standing just behind me paying closer attention than strangers usually do in a crowd this size.

I didn't turn immediately. No need to look jumpy. Instead, I listened: slow, measured breathing, calm and even, cutting through the murmur of orders and steam wands with a stillness that felt almost deliberate. The space around that presence seemed to part naturally, as though the chaos respected it enough to make room.

When I finally glanced over my shoulder, my stomach performed a small, ridiculous flip.

He was impossible to miss. Tall, sharply dressed in a charcoal suit that looked tailored to the inch, his skin a rich bronze that spoke of warmer climates or careful sun. His jawline was a clean, decisive line that could have been carved from marble, and his eyes—dark amber, steady, far too focused to be accidental—met mine with a calm, unhurried interest that felt almost intentional.

He smiled. Not broadly, not performatively. Just a faint tug at one corner of his mouth, the kind of expression that suggested he already knew several things: about me, about the room, about himself most of all.

I turned back around quickly, heat rising in my cheeks, suddenly aware of my own breathing.

"Long line today," I muttered, mostly to myself, the words slipping out like a reflex.

His voice answered from behind me, warm and smooth as poured honey. "No worse than usual. But some people handle it better than others."

I blinked. Was he speaking to me?

I half-turned. "Handle it better? How exactly does one—"

He nodded toward my hands, which were clasped loosely in front of me. "You're patient. No sighing, no eye-rolling. Unlike the gentleman three spots ahead who looks like he'll die without his fix."

"Oh." An awkward laugh escaped me. "Yeah. Well… I don't drink coffee."

A brief, considering pause.

His eyebrows lifted slightly, amusement flickering in those amber eyes.

"You don't drink coffee?"

"Not even a sip."

He tilted his head, studying me the way one might examine a rare, mildly fascinating specimen.

"Then why are you in Starbucks?"

"For the spiritual experience," I deadpanned.

He laughed—actually laughed. A low, warm sound that seemed to surprise him as much as it did me, rich and unguarded for a single heartbeat.

I liked it more than I expected to.

"And what spiritual experience comes from standing in line for bean water you have no intention of drinking?" he asked, the teasing gentle but unmistakable.

"I'm here for the Iced Peach Oolong Tea."

He blinked once, processing. "You're serious."

"Very."

"Of all the beverages on that board behind the counter, you choose the one that tastes like summer and optimism."

"It does taste like optimism," I said, a touch defensive now. "And joy. And light. And—"

"And no caffeine," he finished lightly.

"I'm sensitive to caffeine. My heart starts racing like it owes someone money."

He laughed again, softer this time, the sound settling somewhere warm in my chest.

"Fair enough. I suppose tea suits you."

"Suits me how?" I asked, curiosity overriding caution.

But he didn't answer right away. He simply watched me for a beat longer than necessary—as though weighing whether to voice whatever thought had just crossed his mind.

Before I could figure it out, the barista's voice cut through: "Next!"

I stepped forward, placed my order, and tried—mostly unsuccessfully—not to overthink the attractive stranger still standing behind me. At the pickup counter, I pulled out my phone and scrolled aimlessly, a shield against further conversation.

When my name was called, I reached for the cup—

—and so did someone else.

Our hands brushed. The drink was cold to the touch, but I felt his warm, steady, electric pulse.

"Sorry. Looks like they mixed up the pickup order."

He handed me my drink as if he'd been waiting for the moment.

"Nathan," he read from the side of the cup, saying my name like it already carried weight, like he'd been practicing it quietly.

"And you are…?" I managed.

He extended a hand—strong, warm, confident.

"Gabriel."

Just Gabriel.

When our palms met, something inside me sparked to life— something old and star-shaped, a childhood wish I thought I'd buried long ago beneath layers of caution and compromise.

"Nice to meet you, Gabriel," I said, striving for calm.

"You as well," he replied.

But his eyes held far more than politeness: interest, amusement, and a quiet recognition I couldn't quite name.

We walked out of the café in different directions, the morning light slanting through the glass doors, and yet I couldn't shake the certainty that something important had just begun—in the middle of a crowded Starbucks, of all unlikely places.

What I didn't know—what I couldn't possibly have known— was that Gabriel Aiden Michaels wasn't merely another handsome face in line. In time I would learn he owned the building where I worked, the company that signed my checks, and more than thirty-six other enterprises scattered across continents, along with properties too numerous to count.

And for reasons still hidden from me…

He had already decided I was worth noticing.

(3) Maniac Weekend

My tech customer service job training was going fine—"fine" in the way something is when you're learning fast enough to keep up, but not so fast that you feel confident yet. We were memorizing new terms, navigating customer scenarios, and pretending we'd never raised our voices at hiccups in internet reception before.

The room was a rotating cast of personalities, nerves, caffeine addictions, and forced introductions, but within the first week, I felt myself quietly gravitating toward two people in particular: Hailey and Marcus. It wasn't dramatic. It never is. It was just that easy sense that some people give off—the ones who feel familiar before they actually are.

Hailey had this buoyant, unapologetic energy, as she walked into rooms already mid-conversation with life. Marcus was sharper around the edges, sarcastic, observant, the kind of guy who pretended not to care while clocking "everything". During those first introductions, when we went around the room sharing names and awkward fun facts, I noticed how naturally conversation flowed when the three of us ended up speaking. That sense cemented itself a few days later when both of them sidled up next to me during a break, grinning as they'd rehearsed it.

"So," Hailey said, eyes flicking over my outfit, "is this your 'week-one professional look' or your 'every-week' look?"

Marcus didn't miss a beat. "Bold choice," he added, nodding at my shirt as it had personally offended him.

I glanced between them, then down at Marcus's Looney Tunes tie and Hailey's Madonna-inspired top—lace, attitude, and all—and smiled.

"Oh please," I said. "I didn't realize it was *Cartoon Network* meets Blonde Ambition Day."

They both laughed, and just like that, the ice cracked, the test passed, and bonds of wit formed. From then on, we ate lunch together most days—sometimes in the breakroom, sometimes at Taco Bell when we needed to feel something again like a holy cleansing. We talked about where we came from, the families that shaped us, goals that scared us, and dreams that felt too big to say out loud. I was more reserved than they were, careful about what I shared, but they were perceptive in that annoying, dead-accurate way.

At some point, Hailey just looked at me and said, casually, "So… you're gay, right?"

I didn't deny it. I wasn't ready to lie, either.

"Yep. Ya caught me. I'm platonically gay." I said with a southern drawl.

Marcus nodded, unfazed. "Cool," he said. Then, after a beat, added, "But I'm not gay, so… don't. Just—don't go there."

"Duly noted," I replied, more serious in tone trying to get off the topic and that was that. No drama. No awkwardness. Just boundaries, honesty, and the quiet relief of being accepted without being examined.

By the end of the week, we were already a unit—inside jokes, shared eye-rolls during training videos, a rhythm that felt earned faster than it should have.

Then one evening, as we packed up to leave, the universe decided to be funny.

Normally, we peeled off in different directions, and I assumed they lived elsewhere or had stops to make before heading home. But that night, for the first time, we all exited together and walked the same route.

I joked, "So… you guys coming to check out where I live or what?"

"Nah, man," Marcus said. "I live just about two blocks down this road."

"Seriously?" Hailey blurted. "I do too. Candlewick Apartments?"

"Yeah," Marcus and I chorused. "Me too" we both said in unison and then we chuckled.

She smiled. "Interesting… let's see how this plays out."

A few minutes later, we arrived at the same building. Same floor. Doors just yards apart. It felt ironic, almost staged—the kind of coincidence you don't question because it already feels inevitable.

"See you later, neighbors," we called, all of us half-leaning out of our doorways.

And that's how our first—and second—week really began. We visited each other often, borrowed things, ate dinner together, watched movies and shows, and spent more than a few nights glued to WWE. On Thursday evenings, we hit a small gym near the corner, overworked the treadmills, and half-heartedly committed to light aerobics. But the best moments were when we planned major TV events to binge, paired with good old-fashioned comfort food—the kind that made a place feel like home.

Eventually, those plans grew bigger than whatever we already had in our kitchens—and that's when logistics entered the friendship.

The grocery store near our building was closed for renovations, which honestly made sense, because it looked like it had been built in 1997 and never emotionally recovered. It used to be our go-to place for decent rotisserie chickens, but since Hailey had declared my apartment the official WrestleMania Viewing Headquarters, we needed supplies *now*, and the next closest store was five or six miles away.

WrestleMania requires a mountain of food—the kind of food young adults buy when trying to mask emotional instability with snacks—so we had to take Marcus's car if we wanted any hope of fitting it all. It was technically my day to drive, which also meant it was my designated day to fill the gas tank and fund most of the groceries. Fine. I accepted my fate.

Marcus's car—a 1990 Saturn S-Series four-door compact—wasn't the worst thing on wheels, unless you counted the A/C, which had a habit of spitting out puffs of dust like we were summoning ancient spirits. Luckily, today was mild enough that rolling the windows down felt almost intentional.

When we finally pulled into the parking lot, it was a mad dash to find a cart that didn't have a wobbly, possessed wheel. Marcus pushed the cart like it weighed twelve regrets. Hailey read the shopping list in the tone of a general preparing for war. And I was already a little worn out from a day of partial internet surfing, muffin-making, Amazon impulse shopping, and YouTube remix dancing.

"Okay," she said, eyes scanning the list, "we need: wings, chips, salsa, rotisserie chicken, mozzarella sticks, ice cream, soda, sweet tea—"

"That's a cardiologist's nightmare," Marcus muttered.

"It's WrestleMania," Hailey declared. "Our hearts know the risk."

I grabbed a family-size bag of cheese puffs. "This is necessary."

"For who?" Marcus deadpanned. "A family of raccoons?"

"Me," I said.

Hailey laughed her signature cackle. "Nathan eats his feelings. Respect."

We turned down the freezer aisle, and that's when I felt it.

That subtle shift in the air again.

That… presence.

Nothing dramatic. Just familiar.

I glanced toward the end of the aisle.

A man in a charcoal suit stood there, studying boxes of frozen dinners like he was evaluating a portfolio. Dark bronze skin. A sharp profile. Posture too deliberate to belong in a freezer section. He didn't rush. He didn't fidget. He simply *was* composed, contained, out of place.

My stomach tightened. I blinked.

He wasn't looking at me, but something about the angle of his shoulders, the stillness of him, the quiet authority he carried— No. It couldn't be.

Gabriel would never shop here. His suit alone probably cost more than my rent.

"Dibs on Mozza sticks!" Hailey shouted, grabbing two boxes and nearly taking me out at the knees.

When I steadied myself and looked back, the man was still there.

This time, he lifted his head slightly, as if aware of being observed, though his gaze never quite met mine. Just a fraction of acknowledgment. Enough to unsettle me.

Hailey followed my line of sight and snorted. "Who you lookin' at? Oh *that* guy? Relax. That's Mr. Cortez."

I froze.

"He manages the Starbucks near our office building," she added casually, tossing a box into the cart. "Total business-bro vibe, right?"

The name landed differently than I expected. Grounded the moment. Disarmed it. When I looked again—

He was gone. Just… gone.

Marcus frowned at me. "You okay?"

"Yeah," I said, a little too fast. "Thought I saw someone I knew."

Hailey shrugged, already reaching for another box. "Happens. Faces repeat. Especially when you're tired."

I nodded, even though I knew that wasn't it. Because whatever that was, it wasn't memory. And it wasn't a coincidence.

"Don't worry," Hailey sang, hopping onto the smooth linoleum. "Someday all your wishes will come true."

She took off down the ice cream aisle lying on the cart, arms stretched wide like airplane wings, boots tiptoeing pushing her faster over the polished floor. For a second—alarmingly—it worked. She was flying. Coasting. Picking up speed.

Then physics remembered her.

She clipped the edge of a shopping cart and launched forward in a heel-over-head flip, her right hand landing inside the other cart for a quick second—just long enough to complete the rotation—before she hit with a thud and skidded across the floor, sliding cleanly under another cart on the opposite side like a cartoon stunt double who hadn't read the safety memo.

"I'm okay!" she called from the linoleum, laughing wildly. "Yippee!"

I stared. Marcus groaned.

Of all people to collide with, it had to be Mr. and Mrs. Dithers.

Mr. Dithers, the customer service manager at work, stared down at us like we'd just personally insulted the concept of grocery store etiquette and shopping order.

"Oh, hello there … Hailey. Nathan. Marcus." He said our names dryly, like bullet points on a complaint form. "Why not watch where you're gallivanting?"

The last word was fired directly at a rumpled Hailey on the floor.

Mrs. Dithers, bless her soft soul, fussed over Hailey and helped her up, murmuring kind things while trying not to stray too far from her husband. Meanwhile, Mr. Dithers was inspecting the squashed loaf of white bread with the Hailey hand logo pressed into it like it was a crime scene.

He sighed loudly. "Now I must retrace my steps and replace this 'loaf disaster'. Completely unacceptable."

He turned the cart around with great martyr energy and wheeled off, still muttering about "careless youths" and "ruined bread."

Mrs. Dithers was patting his arm and shuffling as fast as she could, trying to console him.

Marcus and I just stood there, mouthing and whispering little "sorrys at their retreating backs. It did absolutely nothing to fix the situation.

"Great," I muttered. "Now we're going to be his little office puppets. He's going to have us fetching his coffee and doughnuts for the next six months."

"No," Marcus said darkly. "He'll ask us to cut up his steak and feed him each piece. And Hailey over there will be required to shine his shoes or—worse—massage his feet."

"Ew, hell no!" Hailey gasped. "I'm not going anywhere near that man's lower extremities. He already reeks of Old Spice or Old Man, whichever it is, and that alone makes me throw up in my mouth a little when he walks behind me at work."

"Didn't your dad ever wear Old Spice?" I asked, weirdly curious. Mine had.

"Nah. Maybe Aqua Velva or some bargain-bin knockoff," she said. "It was okay, I guess. He was the one who got me into WWE. Of course, it wasn't called WWE back then. It was something else."

Marcus, human trivia machine, chimed in immediately.

"'What is the WWF?' Alex," he said in a fake game-show voice.

"That's right, Marcus — 400 points have been added to your score," the fake-voiced Alex replied.

Hailey rolled her eyes so hard I worried for her retinas. I nudged the cart forward a little faster, forcing Marcus to catch up as we neared the magazine rack.

"Oh, oh—the latest *People* magazine is out!" Hailey yelped, bouncing back as if nothing happened and snatching a copy off the shelf.

Hailey flipped open her magazine before I could even blink.

"Top 100 Sexiest Men of the Decade," she announced dramatically.

"Don't tempt me," I muttered, already reaching for my own copy. Too late.

On the cover were men so genetically blessed they should've been illegal. I flipped through the first few pages, eyes widening at jawlines, smiles, shoulders—everything sculpted by either flawless genes or divine favoritism.

"Oh my God…" I whispered, stopping on a photo spread. "Where do they grow these men? What state? Whose farm? What time of day are they released? And what, exactly, do I have to do to look like him?"

Hailey snorted, flipping through her own issue. "Please. Half of them probably drink imported glacier water harvested by monks."

I laughed, leaning on the cart as I kept flipping. "I would happily be a houseplant in that glacier monastery."

While I ogled—purely as a mental health exercise, of course— Hailey suddenly went quiet.

Not her playful quiet. Not her dramatic quiet.

A sinking quiet.

I looked over.

She wasn't in the *Sexiest Men* section anymore. She'd stopped at a pull-quote:

"I had a crush I couldn't shake… and it cost me my marriage." — Actor's tell-all interview.

Hailey's jaw tightened. Her fingers curled slightly around the glossy page, the paper faintly crinkling under the pressure.

"You okay?" I asked softly.

She blinked a couple of times, forcing a small laugh. "Yeah, I just—ugh. Stuff like this annoys me."

I tilted my head. "What part?"

"The part where people ruin families because they can't control themselves," she said, closing the magazine a little too firmly. "It's selfish. And stupid. And—"

Her voice wobbled.

That's when I knew: this wasn't about the actor.

"Hey," I murmured.

She exhaled shakily. "My dad… he did something like this."

Marcus, three feet behind us, was flipping through a magazine about building miniature cities, absolutely oblivious as he walked. (How he didn't hit a single shelf was a mystery worthy of documentary study.)

Hailey kept talking, eyes unfocused on the magazine racks.

"I was fifteen," she said quietly. "My parents seemed fine. Normal fights, but nothing major. Then suddenly he's gone. Turns out he'd been talking to some woman online for months. Mom found out. He left two days later."

My chest tightened — not with shock, but with recognition. The kind that settles low and heavy.

"Hailey…"

"They divorced before Christmas. He didn't even come to my sixteenth birthday the following summer. And every time I see stories like this—" She gestured vaguely with the magazine. "— it hits the same stupid old bruise."

I placed a hand on her arm. She didn't pull away.

"You're allowed to hurt," I said as we stopped. "Even ten years later. Pain doesn't care about expiration dates."

She gave a small, watery laugh. "Thanks, Nathan."

We stood there for a second longer than necessary, the hum of the freezers now filling the space between us.

Then we started pushing the cart again — Marcus still trailing behind us, reading about architectural roof supports like he was preserving world peace.

Hailey sighed, wiped her eyes, then abruptly snapped the model-building magazine out of Marcus's hands.

"Hey!" Marcus protested.

She didn't stop walking—she just *flung* the magazine down the aisle with surprising force.

It slid perfectly across the floor and landed at the feet of—you guessed it…Mr. Dithers. Again. Hands on hips. The human storm cloud. He looked at Hailey like she'd just murdered a Shakespearean literary work.

She threw her hands up. "Sorry! Sorry! Emotional moment!"

He grumbled something about "youthful dramatics" and bent to pick it up. The look he gave us promised future suffering.

We fled.

By the time we reached the checkout line, our cart looked like we were feeding an army of unhealthy teenage wrestlers. The conveyor belt groaned under the weight of wings, chips, sodas, dips, cereal, hot sauce, beef jerky, and enough frozen appetizers to destabilize the economy.

Marcus suddenly perked up.

"Ooh! Chocolate bars!"

He reached for one like it was calling him home.

Hailey smacked his hand. "No!"

"What—why?" he demanded.

"Because," she said firmly, "if you get that now, you don't get any of my chocolate chip cookies this weekend."

Marcus froze. The betrayal was immense.

"You wouldn't," he whispered.

"I would," she said, dead serious.

He slowly, dramatically, put the chocolate bar back. Then crossed his arms like a scolded eight-year-old.

I leaned toward the cashier—who looked alarmingly younger than us—and I said, "Kids… am I right?"

She did not laugh.

I slid my debit card out of my Velcro wallet and reconsidered my life choices.

As we were leaving the store sometime later, Marcus muttered an "Unbelievable" behind Hailey as the automatic doors whooshed open.

And then—because emotional maturity is optional—he tapped, maybe slapped, her shoulder.

"You're IT!"

Hailey shrieked and bolted. Marcus took off ahead of her at a breakneck pace, both of them sprinting through the parking lot like sugar-high children with car keys.

I watched them run, all while shaking my head and muttering to myself about being morons.

"I'm with freakin' kids," I said aloud, trudging after them toward the car. "Actual children from the old neighborhood used to do this crap."

But the smile on my face said otherwise…these two were my emotional support baggage.

Loading the car turned into a competitive sport. Marcus started stacking frozen pizzas vertically like skyscraper developments. Hailey wedged chip bags around them as "structural cushioning." I slid the rotisserie chickens in like puzzle pieces while narrating everything in a dramatic sports announcer voice.

"And Nathan slides the chicken into the back slot—perfect placement! Look at that spacing! Look at that confidence!"

"Shut up," Hailey laughed, though she was grinning hard. She angled a case of soda into the last remaining gap. "Boom. Tetris – End Game."

The trunk closed with an unsettling crunch that sounded suspiciously like a crushed box of cupcakes, but none of us dared check.

Hailey exhaled, leaning back against the car. "Hey," she said softly, nudging me with her elbow. "Thanks… you know. For listening earlier."

"Always," I said. "You don't have to carry that alone."

She gave a genuine smile. The kind that wasn't loud or sarcastic or jokey. Just real. It hit me right in the chest.

Then Marcus ruined the moment by bouncing on his toes like a caffeinated toddler.

"Uh… guys?" he whispered. "I need to go back in."

Hailey groaned. "Marcus—NO. We're not doing round two."

"It's important," he hissed.

"What could possibly—"

He bolted.

Just took off running like the last golden ticket to Willy Wonka's factory had dropped somewhere near aisle seven.

Unfortunately, Mrs. Dithers chose that exact moment to exit with a full cart.

Marcus swerved at the last second, arms pinwheeling, and missed her by maybe three inches.

Mrs. Dithers shrieked — a sound sharp enough to summon paramedics.

"Oh my gosh, I am *so* sorry!" I called, mortified.

She waved me off but clutched her pearls as she'd narrowly escaped a runaway bull.

Hailey pressed her palms to her face. "We are *literally* banned from all future promotions at work. We're done. Finished. Fired before hired."

We waited.

Marcus did not return.

Which was… concerning.

Hailey and I leaned against the trunk again, shoulders brushing. The parking lot noise faded into background hum.

She let out a slow breath.

"Everything changed so fast," she said quietly. "After the divorce."

I stayed silent.

"Mom had to find a job overnight. She'd never worked outside the house before. But she did it. She survived. We survived."

She paused.

"And my dad…"

Her voice cracked.

I waited.

"He became someone else," she said. "Someone mean. Someone who yelled more than he talked. One day he threatened my mom — right there in the kitchen. Me and my brother were coming home from school. We heard everything through the door."

A tear slid down her cheek.

She wiped it quickly. Too quickly.

And it hit me like a punch.

"He went from being this gentle guy," she whispered, "to a straight-up WWE villain. The kind you boo before you even see him."

I nodded, throat tight. "I'm sorry. Truly."

She sniffed. "I'm okay now. Mostly. Just… some emotional bruises stick around longer than physical ones."

We stood there together…in quiet respect for her feelings.

Until the sliding doors whooshed open.

Out stomped Mr. Harmond, the grocery manager.

He was holding Marcus by the elbow like a kindergarten teacher escorting a rule-breaker.

Marcus looked… guilty.

Extremely guilty.

Mr. Harmond lifted a plastic bag in his free hand. Inside were three empty candy-bar wrappers and three unopened bars.

"Did you lose this?" he snapped. "Or *him*?"

Hailey and I exchanged a look.

"He owes us," Mr. Harmond continued, voice booming, "for three candy bars out of the six he ate."

Hailey choked on air.

I covered my mouth.

Marcus whispered, "They were samples."

"They were *not* samples," Mr. Harmond thundered. "They were inventory."

Hailey pinched the bridge of her nose. "Marcus. You absolute menace."

"I panicked!" Marcus whispered. "You said no chocolate! My childhood instincts took over!"

Mr. Harmond sighed, suddenly very tired. "Please pay. And kindly never bring him in unsupervised again."

"We won't," Hailey and I said in unison.

We paid. We apologized. We bowed like remorseful tourists.

As we finally herded Marcus toward the car, I muttered,

"I really am hanging out with actual children."

Marcus shrugged. "Children don't eat six candy bars."

"Exactly!" Hailey barked. She grabbed the remaining three and shoved them into her purse.

"These are *mine*."

Marcus opened his mouth to protest. One look from Hailey shut him down completely.

And somehow —this group, chaotic as it was, felt like home.

(4) Hailey & Marcus

Hailey POV

People assume I've always been like this—loud, fearless, unfiltered. Like I came out of the womb with sarcasm and eyeliner and a soundtrack playing behind me. But confidence, real confidence, is something you *build* when the ground under you keeps shifting.

My dad left when I was fifteen.

That's the clean version. The polite version.

The messier truth is that he didn't just leave—he changed. He got louder. Meaner. Words turned sharp. Threats slipped into conversations as they belonged there. He started blaming my mom for everything that didn't go right in his life, and when you're a kid watching that happen, you learn something early: love isn't always safe.

College was supposed to be my escape. And in some ways, it was. I dyed my hair. Cut classes. Fell in love with the idea that I could be anyone if I just didn't go home. I partied hard, rebelled harder, and pretended freedom didn't come with consequences. But freedom without structure gets lonely fast.

So when I landed in a call center—headset, scripts, corporate smiles—I laughed at the irony. Me. Following procedures. De-escalating angry strangers. Being told when I could take a bathroom break.

But here's the thing no one tells you: stability feels radical when chaos is your baseline.

The call center wasn't my dream. It was my truce with adulthood. It paid rent. It gave me health insurance. It let me breathe. And somehow, between calls and canned empathy, I learned how to be strong without being loud all the time.

I still glide down grocery store aisles like I'm invincible. But now I know exactly why I need to.

When I first noticed Nathan, I clocked him as quiet. Not shy—there's a difference—but contained, like someone who's learned to keep things folded neatly inside. He dressed like he was trying to be professional before he was comfortable, and he watched people more than he spoke. That kind of silence usually means one of two things: judgment… or depth.

I tested him early. Teased him about his clothes. Poked the edges. Most people either shrink or snap back too hard.

He did neither.

He fired back—clean, funny, precise. Not mean. Not defensive. Just *present*. That told me more than any introduction ever could.

I also noticed he listened. Really listened. When people talked about themselves, he didn't wait for his turn—he absorbed. Filed away details. Reacted later, thoughtfully. That's rare. Especially in a room full of people trying to be noticed.

Somewhere between Taco Bell lunches and shared eye-rolls during training videos, I decided something: Nathan wasn't fragile. He was *layered*.

And layered people? They're worth keeping close.

So yeah. I decided early on—I wanted him in my circle. Not to fix. Not to save. Just to walk beside. Because people like him don't always ask for friendship… but they notice when you offer it.

Marcus POV

I don't talk about my past much. Not because it's dark—just because no one ever asked.

People think I'm guarded because I don't care. The truth is I learned early that talking doesn't always change anything. So I got good at listening instead.

My parents stayed together, technically. Same house. Same last name. But emotionally? Two people orbiting the same space, careful not to collide. There were rules. Expectations. Be practical. Be realistic. Don't dream too loud.

College was my rebellion—but it didn't look like Hailey's.

I skipped classes to work. Took jobs I hated because they paid. I told myself I was being responsible while quietly resenting everyone who got to "find themselves." I didn't party much. Didn't break many rules. My rebellion was choosing survival over passion and pretending it was a choice I liked.

When I ended up in customer service, it felt… fitting. Safe. Predictable. I knew how to manage people's disappointment. I'd been practicing my whole life.

But something changes when you realize you're *good* at something you never wanted. You start wondering if you settled—or if you adapted.

Working a call center stripped me down in ways college never did. You hear people at their worst. Angry. Afraid. Small. And you learn how to stay calm without disappearing. How to hold boundaries without becoming cold.

I'm not chasing some big dream. I'm chasing peace. Consistency. A version of myself that doesn't flinch when life gets loud.

And somehow, in that fluorescent-lit training room, with Hailey cracking jokes and Nathan quietly observing everything—I found people who didn't need me to perform.

That felt new.

Nathan wasn't loud enough to ignore, but he wasn't obvious enough to read either.

At first, I couldn't figure him out. He didn't posture. Didn't overshare. Didn't complain just to fill space. In a call center full of people performing versions of themselves, that stood out.

What caught my attention wasn't what he said—it was *when* he spoke. He waited. Observed. Then dropped a comment that landed exactly where it needed to. No wasted words. No unnecessary noise.

When Hailey started joking with him, I watched how he handled it. Most people either try to match her chaos or retreat from it. Nathan stayed steady. Matched her humor without losing himself. That takes confidence that most people don't realize they have.

I also picked up on something else: he carried himself like someone who'd been through things he didn't advertise. Not broken. Not bitter. Just… seasoned.

I respect that.

So when it became clear we were forming a little group, I didn't hesitate. Nathan wasn't someone you tolerated—he was someone you *chose*. The kind of person who would show up when it mattered, even if he didn't announce himself doing it.

Those are the people you keep.

Nathan POV

People tend to mistake quiet for uncertainty. I used to let them.

The truth is, I learned early that words have weight. That once you say something, you can't always take it back — and sometimes it gets used against you. So I became selective. Not withdrawn. Just careful.

I didn't come into the call center looking for a connection. I came looking for footing. A place where I could show up, do the job, collect the paycheck, and not be asked too many questions about who I was or where I was headed. After years of recalculating myself to fit rooms that weren't built with me in mind, stability felt like mercy.

Training week was a blur of scripts, laminated flowcharts, and people trying too hard to prove they belonged. Everyone had a version of themselves they were auditioning. Loud confidence. Forced charm. Manufactured relatability.

I stayed still.

That's when Hailey noticed me.

She clocked me fast — not as weak, but as contained. I could tell by the way she teased: light, intentional, testing for response rather than reaction. When she joked about my clothes, it wasn't mean. It was an invitation.

So I answered.

Not defensively. Not cruelly. Just honestly. Humor where humor belonged. Boundaries where they mattered. I didn't need to win — I just needed to be present.

She respected that immediately.

Marcus took longer to read, but I saw him before he knew he was being seen. He listened the way people do when they've learned that talking doesn't always change outcomes. He absorbed the room. Measured responses. Filed things away. That kind of attentiveness doesn't come from apathy — it comes from adaptation.

Somewhere between icebreakers and bad coffee, Taco Bell lunches and shared looks during corporate videos, something unexpected happened.

I relaxed.

Not dramatically. Just enough to stop bracing.

With them, I didn't have to explain myself or perform a version of who I was supposed to be. I could be thoughtful without being invisible. Quiet without being overlooked. Present without being exposed.

I didn't tell them everything. Not then. But I noticed how they handled silence. How neither of them rushed to fill it or interrogate it. That mattered more than any confession.

I'd spent a long time learning how to survive on my own. What I hadn't learned yet was how to let people walk beside me without flinching.

Hailey and Marcus made that feel possible.

So when the lines between coworkers and something more began to blur, I didn't resist it. I didn't overthink it. I simply stayed.

Sometimes, that's how trust begins — not with declarations, but with consistency.

Together

None of us said it out loud at the time, but we'd all landed in the same place for different reasons. Rebellion. Survival. Recovery.

A call center wasn't where we planned to end up, but it was where we learned who we were becoming.

None of us knew it yet—not really—but those first impressions sealed something quiet and lasting. We didn't just fall into friendship.

We recognized each other, and that was totally enough to move into life with each other.

(5) Summer Fun & Memories

The sun was bright enough to make the dashboard gleam, and the breeze pouring through the cracked windows felt like early-summer freedom. The car hummed beneath us, full of groceries, stolen hope, and several crushed cupcakes I was too afraid to check.

Then the radio crackled.

A guitar riff blared, followed by the roar of a roller coaster and kids screaming in the background.

"SIX FLAGS SUMMER BLAST IS HERE!" the announcer shouted with Olympic-level enthusiasm. "Buy TWO tickets and get ONE FREE! This MONTH only!"

Marcus transformed instantly into a two-ton toddler. He slapped the roof of the car, bounced in his seat, and shouted, "CAN WE GO?! Hailey! Nathan! PLEASE tell me we can go!"

Hailey and I exchanged a long, parental glance. The kind where both parents silently agree on the same regrettable decision.

"It *would* be fun…" Hailey admitted.

"After all these years?" I shrugged. "It'd be kind of perfect."

"But Saturday's the wrestling event…" she remembered.

I grinned. "So? We go on Sunday."

Marcus cheered as if he'd just won the Royal Rumble.

Hailey pointed a finger at both of us. "You guys realize we'll be dragging into work Monday morning, right?"

"It'll be worth it," Marcus said.

"And nothing major ever happens on Mondays," I added.

Which was, historically speaking, the kind of sentence that tempts fate.

The conversation turned into a nostalgia parade—every ride we remembered, every snack that ruined a childhood stomach, every time Marcus allegedly threw up on a stranger (he said it happened once; Hailey guessed it was four times; I decided not to pick sides).

Then Marcus got quiet.

"You guys remember Iron Wolf?" he asked.

Hailey groaned. "The standing coaster? Absolutely not."

"That's the one," Marcus said, leaning forward like he was about to tell a ghost story.

We listened.

"So, I'm maybe… thirteen? And they sat this really heavy guy beside me. Like… borderline too heavy to ride. The workers almost turned him away, but his mom made a whole scene, so they let him stay."

Hailey and I leaned in, wide-eyed.

"Okay, so the ride starts. Everything's fine. Then—thirty seconds in—the guy PASSES OUT. Just—gone. Slumped. His body is bouncing against the shoulder harness like a rag doll."

"Oh my gosh…" Hailey whispered.

"And then," Marcus said grimly, "we hit the loop."

I swallowed.

He nodded. "Yep. He slipped. Slid halfway past the seat. Fell into the safety net while the coaster was still moving."

"NO WAY," I said, horrified.

Marcus shuddered. "He survived, but he was hurt badly. I've never forgotten it."

Hailey pointed a frozen finger at him. "I am *not* going on that ride."

"That was ten years ago!" I said. "I'm sure they improved it."

"I am not your crash-test dummy, Nathan."

I held up a hand. "Okay, okay. No Iron Wolf."

Marcus nudged her shoulder gently. "We'll keep you safe. Like your older brothers."

Hailey softened. Her voice dropped. "You know what? I actually… believe that. You two are kind of the family I didn't expect to find."

My heart squeezed a little.

I smiled at her. "Right back at you."

<hr>

We passed a cluster of billboards—bright colors, loud fonts, promises nobody believed.

The first was for our tech company. Mr. Dithers was front and center, arms crossed, forehead creased like a man personally fighting crime through customer service metrics. Behind him stood Mr. Emerson, our VP, looking far more photogenic.

Hailey groaned. "Why isn't Emerson in front? He's the one with the face you'd actually trust to fix your Wi-Fi."

"Because," I said, "Dithers probably bribed the marketing team with coupons."

Next billboard: A stunning Tuscan-themed restaurant with warm lighting, wine glasses sparkling in candlelight.

Gabriel's Sogno Toscano 3 Michelin Stars.

There it was again— that name.

Gabriel.

For half a second, my stomach did a small, traitorous swirl.

A coincidence. It had to be.

Unless… he *did* own a restaurant? Or several? Or the whole city? Or—

"Three Michelin stars!" Marcus said. "I bet that place costs more than my rent."

Hailey snorted. "A coworker said the waiting list is seven months. They only serve two meals a day. You need a *reservation* to breathe near the door."

The waiter on the billboard was hot. Which, frankly, felt rude.

I stared until Hailey snapped the thought with a smack to my arm. "Don't even think about it."

"I wasn't!" I lied.

We drove on.

The last billboard advertised a "$14,999 Bathroom Remodel — COMPLETED IN SIX HOURS!"

I scoffed. "Yeah, and I can build the Eiffel Tower with Popsicle sticks."

"Impossible," Hailey said, shaking her head. "You need at least two days just for tile curing!" I added.

"Fraud!" Marcus declared.

We all nodded like informed contractors.

I pulled into the underground parking garage and eased into Marcus's usual spot. The engine ticked itself quiet, and before I could even unbuckle my seatbelt, Marcus groaned dramatically.

"Dude… there are so many bags. Did we buy out the entire frozen-food section?"

"Yes," Hailey said, already unbuckling her seatbelt. "And you two strong, capable men can take them all upstairs while I—uh—go use the restroom."

She opened the door.

I grabbed her sleeve.

"Oh no you don't."

Hailey froze. "Nathan… when nature calls—"

"This isn't nature," I said calmly. "This is strategy." I narrowed my eyes. "Classic Hailey move. The 'fake bathroom break' to avoid hauling groceries."

Marcus nodded solemnly. "She's used it three times this month."

"I have *not*—okay, maybe twice—"

"Hailey," I said, lowering my voice, "if you don't help unload this car, you get **none** of the food I bought. Not the ice cream. Not the wings. Not even a single mozzarella stick."

"You wouldn't," Hailey gasped, like I'd threatened her bloodline.

"Don't try me," I said, squinting, two fingers pointing from my eyes to hers.

Out of the corner of my vision, Marcus began tiptoeing away like a cartoon criminal.

"And you," I snapped, pointing at him, "are not getting any candy or the dessert Hailey's making this weekend."

He froze mid-sneak. "...Even the cookies?"

"Especially the cookies."

And just like that, both of them returned to the trunk with the obedience of younger siblings who had suddenly realized their survival depended on snacks.

As we unloaded the car, I couldn't help remembering my brothers back home. Same trick. Same tone. Same threat of withheld candy. Worked every time.

Some things never change.

We carried the bags up the stairs—Hailey loudly complaining about gravity, Marcus stopping every landing to rest like a Victorian widow, and me juggling half the trunk like a pack mule.

But honestly?

It felt good.

Stupid and simple and warm.

A day spent shopping, laughing, teasing, reliving old stories, and building new ones. A day that made the city feel less like a maze and more like a home.

When we finally dropped the bags inside my apartment and collapsed on the couch like three exhausted potatoes, I sighed contentedly.

"Today was good," I said.

Hailey nodded. "Really good."

Marcus was already halfway through one of the chip bags. "We should do this more often."

We would've kept the moment going, but then Hailey checked her phone and let out a shocked gasp.

"Uh… guys?" she said. "WrestleMania is now a *two-day* event." We all stared at her.

"WHAT?" Marcus screeched, dropping the chips.

"So Sunday is out?" I asked.

She nodded solemnly. "Six Flags will have to wait for another weekend."

Marcus groaned. "Noooo…"

I leaned back, staring at the ceiling.

"Hey," I said softly, smiling despite everything, "it just means we get to do more stuff together."

Both glanced at me. And in that small, quiet moment, I knew: We weren't just friends. We were forming something like a family. And none of us had seen it coming.

(6) Motorcycle at Dusk & Small Victories

For two full days after Starbucks — and then discovering an Italian restaurant bearing his name the following afternoon — I convinced myself Gabriel was already fading into the background of my mind, the way most fleeting encounters do.

The city is good at that. It makes temporary impressions feel permanent for about five minutes before swallowing them whole.

But somehow, he lingered.

In the tone of his voice. In the curve of that half-smile. In the way he'd said my name — not like he was trying it out, but like he already knew it.

I told myself it was harmless. A crush sparked by caffeine-free flattery. Nothing more.

Then, on the drive home Saturday, I saw it.

A billboard. Gold lettering. His name is attached to an Italian restaurant.

I stared at it longer than I should have.

Was it his restaurant? Or just a coincidence? There had to be other Gabriels in the city. Still, the question lingered — quiet, unresolved.

By Wednesday evening — after a long day of training calls and not nearly enough sleep — I wanted nothing more than to drag myself home, collapse on my couch, and put on something animated enough to reset my nervous system.

The sun had dipped low by the time I reached my building. Orange light spilled across the sidewalk, turning the city into something warm and cinematic. And that's when I noticed it: a sleek, black motorcycle parked beside the curb.

Sleek was an understatement. This thing looked like it was hand-forged by some ancient order of stylish assassins.

A rider sat on it, still as a statue.

Helmet on. Visor down. One hand resting on the clutch. The other was loosely draped on the handlebars.

He wasn't looking at me. Or at anyone. He was just… there.

But there was something undeniably familiar in the way he sat. Not in a recognizable sense—just a sense. A feeling. A whisper of: *Haven't I seen that suit? Haven't I seen those shoulders?*

Of course, the helmet made it impossible to identify anything. Logic told me it was no one I knew.

Still, when I stepped toward the door, the rider suddenly straightened. Not startled—just slightly more alert, like the moment before someone chooses a direction. Then he eased the bike away from the curb and disappeared down the street so smoothly it barely made a sound.

I stood frozen for a few seconds.

"Okay…" I whispered to myself, "That was weird."

But weird doesn't equal significant. Not in a city of nine million.

I went inside telling myself that I'd seen nothing meaningful— just a stranger on a very expensive bike. Still, my mind replayed the outline of that suit jacket. The cut. The shoulders. The posture.

I shook my head. "No way." I absolutely refused to let my brain turn into a conspiracy vending machine.

It wasn't Gabe. It couldn't be.

And even if it was, what would he be doing near my building? He didn't strike me as the "I hang out near modest apartment complexes in the evening" type. More like the "I own buildings, not rent in them" type.

So, I went inside, took a long, grounding shower, and tried not to think about him.

I failed. Completely.

By the time I got into bed, my mind had split into two equally annoying factions:

Faction A: It wasn't him. You're overthinking. You just moved here—your brain is spinning out because you're tired and adjusting.

Faction B: But what if it was him? And if it was, why?

The conservative upbringing in me whispered caution. Suspicion. Fear wrapped in scripture.

The dreamer in me whispered: *Maybe. Maybe he was near for a reason. Maybe this city didn't swallow your star-wish after all.*

I fell asleep in that tug-of-war between hope and doubt, telling myself I'd choose sanity in the morning.

Little did I know — this was only the beginning.

Life had begun forming its own rhythms. Predictable ones. Rhythms that felt comforting, even if they weren't familiar yet.

Wake up. Panic about being late. Realize I'm early. Stand in Starbucks resisting the urge to defend my tea choices before anyone mocks them. Then training, training, training — talking into headsets until my voice went numb.

It wasn't glamorous, but it was mine. A fresh start that tasted like peach oolong and new beginnings.

My apartment building wasn't much, but it held a kind of charm I wasn't expecting — and the people in it carried the same energy. By the third week in the city, I was learning something unexpected: I didn't spiral as hard on the days I wasn't alone especially when I was with the two coworkers who lived on my floor: Hailey and Marcus.

We'd all bonded during the first week of training, mostly over shared exhaustion, fear of failing the onboarding tests, and the mutual belief that the building's elevator was definitely haunted.

Hailey was the kind of girl who could sip coffee like it was gossip. She had a sharp wit, quick eyes, and an emotional intelligence that made her scarily good at reading people. Marcus, on the other hand, was tall, calm, and built like a gentle bouncer who gives you therapy mid-argument.

Together, they made city life feel less like a leap and more like a landing.

Tonight was one of our "small victories" dinners — a new tradition we'd invented to celebrate absolutely nothing except surviving another day of training. Hailey brought tacos, Marcus brought beer, and I brought dessert because my love language is sugar.

We sat in my tiny living room watching some random mystery show that Marcus insisted was "retired detective quality" even though Hailey and I had solved the plot twist eight minutes in.

"You two think you're psychic," Marcus muttered, pointing at the screen. "That's why."

"We're just smarter," Hailey said.

"Speak for yourself," I chimed in. "My superpower is overthinking, not intelligence."

Hailey laughed. "Overthinking is a sign of intelligence."

"Or trauma," I said.

"Both," she replied, raising her beer bottle.

We clinked imaginary glasses. The city felt big, but moments like this made it feel breathable.

About halfway through the episode, when the detective announced the murderer for the hundredth time in the show's history, I cleared my throat.

"Hey… weird question," I said.

Hailey paused mid-sip. "Weird is my love language. Continue."

"Have either of you seen anything—" I struggled for a word that didn't make me sound paranoid. "—odd around the building lately?"

They exchanged a look.

Marcus raised a brow. "Odd how? Ghosts? Creepy neighbor? Another raccoon breaking into the dumpster? Because that raccoon is the size of a toddler."

"No," I said quickly. "Not animals. Just… I don't know… people?"

Hailey tilted her head, studying me. Great. She was entering her therapist mode.

"What happened?" she asked softly.

"I thought I saw someone the other night," I said. "Near the entrance."

Marcus nodded. "A delivery guy?"

"No," I said. "A motorcycle. And the rider kind of looked like… someone I met."

Hailey's eyes sparked. "Ooh, a guy. A *mysterious* guy."

I groaned. "Not mysterious. Just… familiar."

"Was he hot?" she asked bluntly.

"Yes," I answered before I could stop myself.

They both laughed.

"Okay, okay," I said quickly. "It wasn't like that. It was probably just my brain messing with me. I mean, the helmet was down. It could've been anyone."

"Did he approach you?" Marcus asked.

"No."

"Did he follow you?" Hailey added.

"No."

"Did he seductively rev his engine?" Marcus teased.

"Oh my God," I muttered. "No."

"So what made you think it was the same person?" Hailey asked gently.

I shrugged. "I don't know. Something about… the way he held himself. The way he sat. The kind of expensive suit under the jacket."

Hailey raised her brows. "A motorcycle suit? Or a real suit?"

"Real," I said quietly.

She whistled. "Someone's got money."

"Or someone was coming from work," I countered.

"Or someone was checking someone out," Marcus said with a wink.

"Guys," I groaned, burying my face in a pillow. "This is exactly why I didn't say anything."

Hailey nudged my knee with her foot. "You're not crazy, Nathan. City life makes you notice things differently. Shadows look like faces. Strangers look like someone you know. It happens."

"Exactly," Marcus added. "Plus, if he *was* checking you out, you would've felt it. Men like that don't hide."

A strange feeling twisted in my chest. Because that was the thing: I *did* feel something. Not fear. Not attraction alone. More like… alignment. Like noticing someone who had already noticed you.

But I didn't say that.

"That's all," I muttered. "Just making sure I'm not losing it."

"You're not," Hailey said firmly. "But if a hot man in a suit shows up again, try not to run. Introduce yourself."

"Or call us," Marcus added. "We'll do a full background check."

I snorted. "Thanks. I'll keep that in mind."

We laughed again, and for the rest of the night, I tried to shrug off the whole thing. I let myself relax. I ate too many tacos. I let the TV run until the credits blurred into the background.

But later, after they left, and the apartment grew quiet, I stood at the window and looked down at the dim street.

Nothing was there. No motorcycle. No shadows waiting. No sign of him.

And still — I couldn't shake the feeling.

The feeling that *something* had shifted the night I saw that rider.

The feeling that the universe had nudged something out of place.

The feeling that someone out there had noticed me in a way I couldn't explain.

Maybe it was nothing. Maybe it was everything. Maybe it was the beginning.

I just didn't know what.

7) The Envelope I Didn't See Coming

If you'd asked me two and a half weeks into city life whether I believed in fate, I would've answered in a polite but generic Christian way. "God works in mysterious ways." "Yes, the Lord directs our steps." "The universe? I mean, God made it, so sure."

But fate? As in stars aligning? As in doors opening without a doorknob? I would've laughed.

By then, Gabriel was a fading memory — one of those "hot stranger" stories you tell your friends once and then tuck away with the receipts in your junk drawer. I hadn't seen him. Not in my building. Not in the store. Not in any vague helmeted silhouette. Nothing.

Routine swallowed everything.

Wake. Train. Eat. Sleep. Repeat.

The only spark in our repetitive workdays was an upcoming WWE live event at the CitySports Centerplex — and it was all Marcus could talk about. All. Week.

Marcus, Hailey and I were diehard fans in the way only passionate, normal people can be. Cody Rhodes? Legend. Charlotte Flair? Queen. Rey Mysterio? Icon. Goldberg? My childhood hero in a "I pretend to be normal, but my inner kid fainted three times" kind of way.

People in our building knew we were fans of the company called WWE because they could hear our overly animated hooting, hollering, calling, and booing at whatever happened on the screen. Whatever transpired on the screen, we rose to the occasion to imitate on the couch, on the floor, in the hallway, stairwell or elevator. Noise complaints were often filed, and a rookie was usually dispatched to one or all three of our doors to post a noise ordinance violation notice.

So when Hailey scrolled ticket sites obsessively and shrieked, "GUYS, the prices are jumping every five minutes!" it set off the kind of panic usually reserved for natural disasters. We had our doors open to our apartment and were shouting to each other about the prices.

"How much is too much?" she loudly demanded during lunch one day.

"Anything over $75 is too much," I yelled confidently trying to sound like I had standards.

She nearly choked on her soda. "Nathan. That won't even buy us a hot dog in the nosebleed section!"

Marcus groaned and appeared in my doorframe. "Dude, my cousins are coming to town. I already told them we had plans. If we don't go, I'm gonna have to fake a funeral just to avoid running into them while they're in town."

"You can kill off a grandparent," Hailey yelled over.

"I only have one left!" Marcus shouted.

"So, kill that one metaphorically," she yapped.

I rubbed my temples. "We're not killing off family members. We'll just... skip it. It's fine."

"No, it's not fine," Marcus said dramatically. "This is my Super Bowl."

But the tickets sold out. Completely. Utterly. No amount of shouting would cure that.

By Friday, Hailey slammed her laptop shut and said, "The universe hates us." We had all congregated in her apartment, hopeful she could perform magic with the ticket box office. Marcus looked depressed in a way only a sports fan can achieve. And I—I just accepted it with the sad resignation of someone who once believed in star wishes and was trying not to anymore.

We decided to go out for dinner anyway — to mourn our loss like rational adults. The three of us sat outside a tiny Italian bistro, eating too much pasta, complaining about life, and debating which era of WWE had the best promos.

That's when this courier showed up—not some DoorDash kid, but a legit pro in a black cap, all business. She held a thick envelope with my name typed on it in raised ink.

"Are you Nathan Moffett of Crestwick Apartments?" She said my full name — correctly — without hesitation.

"Yes?" I said slowly.

"I need verbal verification. Full name and full address, please?"

I repeated it.

She handed the envelope to me, nodded politely, then walked away. No explanation. No signature needed. She was already on her bike before I could even blink.

Hailey stared at me. Marcus stared at the envelope like it contained backstage passes to heaven.

"What is that?" Marcus asked.

"No clue." My stomach was doing flips.

"Open it!" Hailey shrieked.

"What if it's bad news? Court papers or something?"

"Nathan," she groaned, "no one subpoenas you before dessert. OPEN. IT."

Hands trembling, I tore the seal.

Three glossy cards slid out— black and silver, embossed, heavy.

VIP PASSES — EXECUTIVE LUXURY BOX CITYSPORTS CENTERPLEX — WWE LIVE EVENT ACCESS: CATERED PRIVATE LOUNGE, PREMIUM DRINKS, SIGNED MERCH PACKAGE, LIMO TRANSPORTATION, BACKSTAGE MEET & GREET

Hailey screamed. Marcus actually fell off his chair. The bistro staff came over to try to quiet us down a bit.

My breath left my body in a single, stunned exhale.

"These are…" I whispered, "…real?"

"They're REAL!" Hailey yelled in muffled exclamation.

Marcus grabbed my shoulders. "NATHAN. WHO SENT THESE? SPILL."

"I DON'T KNOW!" I cried back.

He shook me. "WELL, GUESS!"

I tried. I truly did.

But no name was on the envelope. No note. No sender. Just the tickets. Just the impossible.

And for the first time since the motorcycle sighting, since Starbucks, since the half-smile that had lived rent-free in my mind—

I thought of him. Gabriel.

But it was too outrageous, too ridiculous, too delusional to consider.

So I shoved the thought down and let excitement take over.

"We're going!" Hailey screamed, hugging the tickets like they were infused with holy power.

"We're GOING!" Marcus echoed, already pulling up Google Maps like he needed to calculate the limo's orbital trajectory.

"Don't forget, guys—" I said, trying to ride the wave of enthusiasm, "the day *after* this live wrestling event, we're going to Six Flags too. It's gonna be a full weekend of awesome."

Nothing.

They didn't even flinch.

It was like I'd said it to the wind, or maybe to my own reflection. Six Flags was a big deal too—*huge*—but apparently nothing could compete with the intoxicating power of VIP WWE tickets glowing in Hailey's hands.

So I let it go.

And for the next six days, I let myself sink into the thrill of looking forward to something that truly felt like a miracle.

If joy had a sound, it would be the roar inside that arena.

The limo dropped us at a private entrance, and I swear, Hailey started levitating. Marcus nearly cried. I was too busy trying to decide if this was actually happening or if I had died two days ago and never noticed.

The executive box was enormous — plush seating, a catered feast, big screens, a perfect view of the ring. This wasn't just VIP. This was heaven with nachos.

We watched match after match, cheering until our throats burned.

Then, at intermission, something shifted.

From the balcony window of the box, I caught sight of someone backstage. Tall. Clean lines of a bespoke suit. Amber undertone to his skin. Hands shaking the hand of a massive man—

Goldberg. My childhood hero. GOLDBERG.

And there he was.

Gabriel

He clapped Goldberg on the shoulder like they'd known each other since the Attitude Era. Said something. Smiled. Thanked him.

I froze.

He turned.

Our eyes met across the event space.

He winked.

A slow, deliberate, confident wink.

My heart stopped.

He disappeared behind a curtain.

I stood so abruptly that I knocked over a cup.

"Nathan, what's wrong?" Hailey asked.

"I—just—uh—going to get fresh air—be right back—" I bolted.

Down the hall. Past security. Toward the backstage access where I'd seen him.

But by the time I reached the corridor—

He was gone.

No footsteps. No suit. No echo of his presence.

Just a door swinging softly, as if someone had passed through seconds before.

I stood there, breathless and stunned.

"What a coincidence," I whispered.

But it didn't feel like a coincidence.

Not anymore.

When I got back to the executive box, I must've looked like I'd seen the ghost of my childhood dreams because Hailey immediately paused mid–cheese bite and said, "What happened?"

I shook my head and sank into my plush VIP chair. "Nothing," I lied, breathless. "Just a… um… draft."

"A draft?" Marcus deadpanned. "You ran down the hallway like someone stole your kidneys. Drafts don't do that."

I ignored him completely because my heart was still doing Olympic gymnastics.

I saw him. Gabriel. The man whose name I knew only because he said it politely at Starbucks, like he wasn't the most intriguing person I'd met since moving to the city.

And there he'd been. Talking to Goldberg. My Goldberg. The man whose poster I had on my childhood bedroom wall next to a glow-in-the-dark cross and a sticker chart for memorizing Bible verses.

The whole moment felt unreal.

I tried to play it cool. Emphasis on *tried.*

"So," Hailey said suspiciously, setting her plate down, "you're flushed, out of breath, and you look like you saw a miracle. Spill."

"I didn't see a miracle," I said too quickly. "I saw… well… someone."

Marcus leaned forward. "A wrestler?"

"No."

"A celebrity?"

"No."

"A ghost?"

"No."

Hailey narrowed her eyes. "A *guy.*"

"No—yes—no." I covered my face with my hands. "Ugh, I don't know."

When I finally calmed down enough to talk, I said it casually, like it was no big deal:

"I thought I saw someone I knew. That's all."

"You know someone who hangs out backstage with WWE superstars?" Marcus demanded. "WHO are you and WHY are you hiding your connections?"

"I don't have connections!" I snapped.

Then softened. "I mean… I don't *think* I do."

Because the truth was embarrassing:

I didn't know anything about Gabriel. Not his last name. Not his job. Not his background. Not his intentions.

Just his face. His voice. His smile. His stupid wink made half my internal organs retire from service.

And now this —Was he really here?

Or did my brain just paste him onto any attractive man in a suit?

I had no answers.

So instead of spiraling, I did the only sensible thing a sane person would do:

I ate more catered nachos. A lot more. Like, enough to qualify for sponsorship.

Later, when the event ended and we were chauffeured home like royalty with carb-induced brain fog, I kept replaying the moment in my head.

What if it wasn't him? What if I imagined it? Why didn't he wave? Why didn't he say anything? Why did he just wink and disappear? Why did he vanish so fast that it felt supernatural?

And—

Was he the one who sent the tickets?

No. Impossible. That VIP box cost minimum of $15,000, not counting the chauffeur service, the autographed gear, the backstage passes, and the catered buffet that pushed me into the next clothing size.

Who spends that kind of money on three random trainees whose biggest achievement to date was not breaking the office printer?

I tried Googling "WWE VIP anonymous gift etiquette," But even the internet didn't know what to do with my life.

By the time I crawled into bed that night, stuffed, exhausted, and buzzing with leftover adrenaline, I stared at the ceiling for a long time.

A very long time.

"He's not gone," I whispered into the dark.

And it wasn't a romantic statement. It wasn't longing.

It was a realization.

He wasn't gone. Just… elsewhere. Moving in different circles. Living in a world I couldn't imagine.

A world where he could shake Goldberg's hand like it was normal.

A world where sending luxury tickets to strangers was pocket change.

A world I didn't belong to — not yet, maybe not ever.

But the fact remained:

I saw him. He saw me. And he winked.

A stupid, charming, infuriating wink that said nothing and everything at the same time. I turned over in bed and groaned into my pillow.

"Why didn't you just say hi?" I muttered angrily. "You confusing, magical, disappearing… person."

I didn't know if I was excited, confused, flattered, irritated, curious, or all of the above.

Probably all of the above. And when I finally drifted to sleep, it was with one thought echoing in my head:

Someone, somewhere, didn't want me to miss that event.

And someone, somewhere, knew my name.

(8) SIX FLAGS DAY

Early Sunday morning, the day after the wrestling event, Hailey, Marcus, and I piled into the Saturn again and headed toward Six Flags, eventually parking what felt like half a century away from the front gate. Thankfully, a granny-cart tram rolled up before we completely lost hope.

We hopped on and rode toward the gates like three overstuffed tacos—because we *definitely* ate too much during the WWE VIP buffet.

The morning sun was blindingly perfect, the kind of sunshine that makes theme parks feel like magic, cotton candy, and sunscreen. Looney Tunes characters marched around the entrance plaza—Bugs Bunny popping off selfies, Tweety waddling through a crowd, Sylvester giving exaggerated eye-rolls at everyone.

It should've been idyllic.

Except I couldn't get Gabriel out of my head.

Not after last night. Not after that wink. Not after realizing someone with *power* had taken an interest in me, my friends, and apparently my childhood dreams.

Who else could've arranged all of this? Who else even knew enough about me?

Inside the park, the place was alive. Music blasting. Kids were screaming happily. Sun warming every corner of the asphalt.

We were debating which ride to hit first when a group of very muscular humans—men and women—walked past up ahead.

Not normal muscular. The WWE roster displayed muscles through and through. Hailey's jaw dropped. Marcus made a squeak not meant for public spaces.

It was *them.* From last night. Just… strolling around Six Flags like this was a team-building outing.

Some fans rushed up for autographs, others kept a respectful distance. The wrestlers handled it with a mix of charisma, kayfabe seriousness, and occasional sunglasses-hidden exhaustion.

We mingled nearby—rode the coaster next to where a few of them queued up, grabbed drinks, wandered a bit. It was surreal.

Then one of the superstars they called, The Werewolf, glanced at me, did a double take, and walked over.

"You with Gabriel?" he asked casually.

I blinked. "What?"

"You look like the guy Gabriel keeps talking about. Gabriel from Sogno Toscano. Our big sponsor." He nudged Roman Reigns beside him. "Doesn't he look like the guy?"

Roman—yes, actual Roman Reigns—looked me up and down and smirked.

"Oh, hell yeah. Dead ringer. Gabriel's *very* into this one."

My soul left my body.

"I—I don't know what you're talking about," I whispered.

But The Werewolf just laughed softly. "Man, Gabriel never shuts up about you. Says he keeps running into this handsome guy—" he gestures up and down at me— "but he wants a real meeting instead of the 'small chance encounters.' He's infatuated or whatever. It's kinda cute, actually."

Roman folded his arms. "Mutual, huh?"

I spluttered something unintelligible while Hailey and Marcus exchanged looks like they were witnessing divine revelation.

We broke away from the wrestlers after a few more stunned laughs and rode everything except Iron Wolf—Hailey refused on principle after Marcus's near-death flashback story.

But eventually... I felt it.

That awareness. That shift in the air. The sensation of being watched—not scary, not threatening, just… *focused.*

Hailey nudged me as we walked. "You okay? Your face looks weird. Was it the turkey leg? Those things are like sodium grenades."

I leaned closer to her. "I have this feeling… like someone keeps watching me."

Hailey gave me the side-eye. "Nathan. Sweetie. You're being paranoid."

"Am I?" I whispered.

She opened her mouth to respond—but Marcus approached us, waving someone forward.

"Hey," he said brightly, "maybe you can help this guy. Is he looking for something called 'Don Juana Maríame'? I don't see it on the map."

I frowned. "Don Juana… what?"

Marcus stepped aside.

And there he was.

Gabriel stood there as if he'd stepped out of a dream you weren't finished having. Sunlight warmed the bronze in his skin. His shirt sleeves were rolled, casual but deliberate, and the faintest smile tugged at the corner of his mouth. Eyes warm. Smile was faint and devastating.

If the universe had a sense of humor, it was definitely laughing now.

Gabriel nodded once, like we were picking up a conversation we hadn't started yet.

"Hello, Nathan." My name had never sounded so soft or so intentional.

And just like that— Every sound in Six Flags melted into background noise.

Hailey froze beside me. Marcus slowly lifted his soda like a shield. I forgot how breathing worked.

Gabriel glanced at both of them with polite acknowledgment, then returned his attention fully to me.

"I hope I'm not interrupting your day," he said gently.

Hailey elbowed me. Marcus whispered, "He's so tall…"

I cleared my throat. "Uh—we're just… walking. Rides. Theme park things. And—by the way—did you send us the WWE tickets?"

Gabriel's eyes warmed. "I did. Did you enjoy the seats and the event yesterday?" He paused, then added, "Do you mind if I join you on your excursion today? If that's all right."

Hailey nodded so fast her hair nearly flew off. "YES. YES IT IS."

Marcus gave two enthusiastic thumbs up.

I wanted to disappear.

But Gabriel waited—for *my* answer, not theirs.

After a moment, I nodded. "Yes, of course. And thank you so much for your generosity."

His smile grew just a fraction—enough to feel like sunlight landing directly on my chest.

We ended up walking as a group: Marcus rambling about rides, Hailey trying to look normal and failing spectacularly, and me attempting to pretend Gabriel wasn't close enough that our hands occasionally brushed.

Every time it happened, my pulse went sideways.

Hailey whispered loudly, "Act natural."

I whispered back, "I *am* natural."

"You're sweating," she replied.

Gabriel glanced over. "Everything okay?"

"Fine!" I squeaked.

Roman Reigns, who was passing by again, muttered, "Lord help him," and kept walking.

After a few rides and several chaotic near-accidents with Marcus, Gabriel leaned toward me and said quietly:

"Nathan… may I speak with you? Somewhere less crowded?"

My heart hiccupped. "Um… yeah. Sure."

Hailey and Marcus exchanged *this is it* looks and peeled off, giving me "privacy" while absolutely spying from behind a funnel cake stand.

Gabriel and I stepped into a quiet shaded path near the vintage carousel. The sounds of the park softened—spinning rides, children laughing, wind moving through trees.

For the first time since I'd met him, the world felt smaller. Not in a limiting way—But in a way that meant everything had narrowed into this one moment.

He turned toward me fully.

"I hope I haven't made you uncomfortable," he began. "I realize I've appeared… unexpectedly. More than once."

I let out a breath. "You could say that."

He nodded, jaw flexing slightly. "I've been trying to gauge whether I'm overstepping. Whether these… coincidences… are welcomed or intrusive."

The honesty caught me off guard.

"Gabriel," I said softly, "have you really been watching me at work?"

He didn't flinch. "Observing," he corrected gently. "But not in a predatory sense. In a… admiring one. I wanted to understand you before approaching you directly."

I stared. "Why?"

His eyes softened. "Because something about you caught my attention. And once something has my attention… I tend not to ignore it."

My pulse skipped.

"But what were you looking for?" I asked.

"Truth." he said. "I wanted to know who you truly are. How you treat people. What matters to you. And… if your heart was open before I asked it for anything."

The world went quiet.

I swallowed hard. "Well… if you want to know what I'm feeling—" I paused, courage gathering heavy in my chest. "I'm… overwhelmed. Curious. Confused. And—honestly? A little scared."

Gabriel's brow tightened. "Of me?"

"No. Not you." I took a breath. "Of wanting something I'm afraid I'll lose."

Something in his expression shifted—open, vulnerable, listening with his whole being.

"And what is it you want?" he asked.

I looked at him—really looked at him—and let the truth rise.

"I'm looking for a man who treats his parents with deep respect," I said quietly. "Someone who sees his partner as an equal. Someone who honors God—not with loud declarations, but with the way he moves through the world."

Gabriel's breath stilled.

"I'm looking for a man who helps others not out of obligation or applause," I continued, "but because it's right. Because it shows the world what love looks like when it's real."

I hesitated, then added gently, "I'm grateful for the tickets. For the glances." A faint smile tugged at my lips. "And that brings me to something else I'm looking for—presence. Someone willing to walk through life with me, with intention and love. It would have meant something if you'd come in to sit with us last night."

Gabriel swallowed. For the first time since I'd met him, he looked unsteady.

I stepped closer—close enough to see the emotion he was trying, and failing, to hide.

"Love is all of those things," I said softly. "And more. And I believe love conquers everything."

He stared at me as if I'd just handed him the sunrise.

Quietly—almost reverently—he whispered, "I wonder... if I could make you happy."

Something inside me trembled—the kind of tremble that turns into a beginning.

"Gabriel," I said gently, "happiness isn't something you give me. It's something we'd build. Together."

His eyes warmed—slow, bright, transformative.

And then—

Hailey shrieked from behind the funnel cake stand: "OH MY GOD THEY'RE HAVING A MOMENT!"

Marcus added, "CONFESS, NATHAN! CONFESS!"

Gabriel closed his eyes, exhaled, and chuckled. "Your friends," he murmured, "are unforgettable."

"Yeah," I said, smiling, "they're more like family. Sometimes I just wanna send them home early so I can stay out later....alone with someone special."

He looked at me again—steady, certain, hopeful.

"And perhaps," he said quietly, "you could be mine."

Hailey and Marcus pretended (badly) that they weren't eavesdropping anymore. They peeled themselves from behind the funnel cake stand and waved like enthusiastic camp counselors.

"You guys should go ride something!" Hailey called. "Bond! Connect! Kiss— I mean—uh—communicate!"

Marcus saluted. "We'll… uh… give you space!"

They fled. Sort of. They walked ten feet away and then hid behind a merchandise kiosk featuring giant Tweety Bird plushes.

Gabriel watched them go with amused disbelief. "I've hosted corporate board meetings that were less chaotic than your friends."

I grinned. "Yeah. Welcome to my life."

He nodded toward the coaster in front of us. "Would you like to ride this one with me?"

I looked up. It was tall. Fast. Full of screaming people who were definitely rethinking their life choices.

"Uh… sure?"

He offered his hand.

Not to hold. Just to steady me. Just to guide.

But the warmth of it almost buckled my knees.

We boarded the coaster, slipping into the tight seats. The shoulder restraints came down with a decisive clunk. Gabriel's knee brushed mine and stayed there — not touching by accident, but not enough to overwhelm.

Just enough to say: I'm here. You're safe. I'm choosing this moment with you.

As the ride began its slow climb, he leaned closer.

"Nathan," he said softly, "thank you… for your honesty today."

"My honesty?" I repeated.

"Yes," he said. "You spoke of love with more clarity than most people ever will. It moved me."

I swallowed.

The coaster reached the top.

We could see the whole park. Sunlight. Kids. Looney Tunes characters danced near the fountain.

And then—

DROP.

We fell screaming, laughing, shouting. Gabriel's hand gripped the safety bar. Mine accidentally shot over and grabbed his hand tightly.

He didn't let go.

Not for the entire ride.

When we rolled back into the station, breathless and bright-eyed, he didn't release my hand until the safety bar lifted.

Even then, his fingers brushed mine as if reluctant to leave.

The coaster screeched to a halt, and Gabriel was opening his mouth—maybe to say something meaningful, maybe to say something devastatingly attractive—when suddenly:

"SUFFERIN' SUCCOTASH!"

Cartoon chaos descended immediately.

A swarm of costumed characters—Sylvester, Yosemite Sam, Bugs, Daffy, and a very enthusiastic Tweety—swarmed the exit ramp, honking horns, bonking each other with oversized mallets, shrieking in exaggerated cartoon voices, turning what should have been a quiet dismount into a full Saturday-morning episode.

I stumbled backward as the platform tilted under my feet, and my back bumped straight into Gabriel.

His hand found my waist instantly—warm, steady, grounding me before I could even apologize. The contact lasted only a second or two, but it felt longer, like the world had paused just long enough for me to register the heat of his palm through my shirt.

Tweety popped up right in front of us on his little platform, wings flapping, voice pitched to cartoon perfection.

"I TAWT I TAW A WUV BWOOMIN'!"

The crowd around us erupted. Hailey's scream-laugh cut through the noise from somewhere behind the kiosk, high and delighted. Marcus was already waving his phone like evidence in a trial.

"WE JUST WITNESSED THEIR FIRST TWEETY-CERTIFIED RELATIONSHIP!" he bellowed. "And yes, we bought the ride photo to commemorate this historic moment!"

Gabriel let out a slow, quiet exhale—half amusement, half resignation—and glanced down at the glossy printout Marcus thrust toward us.

"Wow," he said softly. "That's... quite the photo."

It really was. The camera had caught us at the steepest drop: faces stretched long from the G-forces, eyes wide and bright with that mix of terror and exhilaration, knees pressed together, hands locked in a death grip, hair whipping straight back like we'd been caught in a wind tunnel. We looked ridiculous and alive and, somehow, unmistakably together.

I felt my face heat up, but I managed a small, sheepish grin.

"Welcome to Six Flags," I said.

Gabriel's gaze flicked from the photo to me, lingering just long enough that my pulse skipped.

"Yeah," he murmured, the corner of his mouth lifting in that familiar almost-smile. "Welcome."

"Welcome to Six Flags," I said.

We drifted toward the midway, the air thick with the smell of fried dough and popcorn, the lights flashing in that dizzying, hypnotic way that makes everything feel a little more alive.

Gabriel slowed at a ring-toss booth, the kind with bottles clustered so tight they look like they're daring you to try. A row of oversized stuffed animals hung overhead like trophies nobody ever wins.

He glanced at me. "You into these?"

I snorted. "Like them? No. They're all rigged. The rings are too light, the bottles too fat at the top."

His mouth curved, that small, knowing smile again. "Then let me try something."

He pulled out his wallet, bought a bucket of rings without hesitation, and stepped up to the line like he was walking into a boardroom instead of a carnival game. His shoulders relaxed, stance balanced, eyes focused in that quiet, deliberate way I was starting to recognize.

He tossed the first ring. It spun clean, landed with a soft clink around the neck of a bottle. The second followed. Perfect arc, perfect landing. The third did the same. Three in a row.

The attendant—a kid maybe nineteen, with a name tag that said "Kyle"—blinked hard, as if his brain had just rebooted.

"Uh… sir? You… you can pick any prize on the top row."

Gabriel didn't even look at the wall of prizes. He just tilted his head toward me.

"It's for him."

My thoughts flatlined for a second.

"Oh—I—uh—"

I scanned the hanging animals quickly, suddenly self-conscious under the bright lights and Kyle's wide-eyed stare. My hand landed on a Snoopy plush wearing tiny aviator sunglasses, looking cool and slightly judgmental.

I pointed. "That one?"

Kyle unhooked it and handed it over. It was heavier than it looked, soft fur, floppy ears, those ridiculous shades perched on his black nose.

Gabriel gave it a once-over, then me. "Suits you."

I hugged the plush to my chest, feeling ridiculous and oddly pleased at the same time. "You were… scarily good at that."

He shrugged, casual as if he'd just tied his shoe. "Aim. Intention. Follow-through."

I raised an eyebrow. "That sounds suspiciously like something from a corporate seminar."

He laughed—low, quiet, the sound settling somewhere warm in my chest. "It is."

We started walking again, Snoopy tucked under my arm like a new sidekick. The midway noise swelled around us—bells, laughter, the distant scream of another coaster drop—but for a second it all felt far away.

Just me, Gabriel, and a stuffed dog in sunglasses who'd somehow become the witness to whatever this was starting to be.

We ended up at one of those sun-bleached picnic tables under a faded red-and-white umbrella, the kind that's probably been here since the park opened. Our trays were piled with overpriced burgers, limp fries still steaming, and sodas sweating rings onto the plastic. Nobody touched the food right away. In the background, another coaster train launched with that signature metallic clank, followed by a wave of screams that sounded half terror, half pure adrenaline.

I pushed a fry around my tray, watching the salt crystals scatter. My heart was doing that annoying flutter thing again.

"Okay," I said finally, forcing myself to look up at him. "I'm about to ask something, and if it's too much, just say so. I'll back off."

Gabriel leaned back a little, hands folded loosely on the table. Calm. Waiting. "Go ahead."

I glanced at Hailey and Marcus. "You two still good with this?"

Hailey mimed zipping her lips shut, then threw away the imaginary key.

Marcus held up his three middle fingers. "Scout's honor. Even though I was never a scout. But yeah, we're good."

I turned back to Gabriel. "I know you're… comfortable. Financially, I mean. And honestly? The numbers don't really matter to me. But people do. And right now it feels like you know way more about me than I know about you."

He didn't argue. Didn't even blink. That silence said enough on its own.

"That's fair," he said quietly.

"So…" I took a breath. "What do you actually do? Day to day. Are you the guy in the boardroom making deals? The one cutting ribbons at groundbreakings? Or the one nobody ever sees?"

He let out a small breath through his nose, almost a laugh without sound. "Definitely not the ribbon guy."

Marcus snorted. "Called it."

Gabriel's mouth curved just enough to show he was amused. Then he looked straight at me. "I build things. Quietly, mostly. Infrastructure projects. Long-term investments. Companies that run fine without my name anywhere on the letterhead."

I tilted my head. "So you're not out there posing for photos at galas?"

"I show up when I have to. I leave as soon as I can."

"That's… very precise."

His eyes met mine. "It has to be."

I hesitated, then went for it. "Do you actually like being wealthy?"

The table went still.

Hailey's eyebrows shot toward her hairline. Marcus froze with his straw halfway to his mouth.

Gabriel didn't flinch. He just held my gaze for a beat longer than felt comfortable.

"I like what it lets me protect," he said after a moment. "And I hate what it attracts."

"Which is?"

"Noise." His voice was even, matter-of-fact. "People who want to be close to the money, not to the person. People who think a big enough check buys them access to everything—including me."

The words landed heavier than I expected.

"So you keep people at arm's length," I said.

"Most people. Yeah."

"Private."

"Very."

I swallowed. My voice came out softer than I meant it to. "Then why me? Why the tickets? Why pay attention at all? Why… look into me?"

His expression didn't change much, but something in his eyes eased—like a door cracking open just enough to let light through.

"I didn't dig to decide if you were 'worthy,'" he said. "I did it to understand how much you carry."

I blinked. "My… weight?"

"How you hold yourself when no one's watching. What matters to you when there's nothing to gain. How you talk about people who can't do anything for you." He paused, choosing his words.

69

"I've learned the hard way to be careful with my time. And with whom I let close."

The word close hung there between us.

I felt my throat tighten. "So this was… like vetting me?"

"Careful curiosity," he corrected, gentle but firm.

Marcus let out a low whistle. "Damn. I've never been carefully curious about anybody. That sounds exhausting."

Hailey kicked him under the table. He winced but shut up.

I studied Gabriel's face—the steady calm, the faint lines at the corners of his eyes that said he'd seen more than he usually let on. "Do you ever show off what you have? Flash it around?"

He shook his head once. "I watched money ruin people growing up. Families. Friendships. Whole lives. Subtlety keeps the important things from breaking."

"So you don't need the spotlight."

"I don't need to be seen," he said. "I need to be sure."

I let that sink in. "And what made you sure… about me?"

He didn't rush the answer. When it came, his voice was quieter than before.

"That you weren't reaching for anything. That you weren't starstruck. That you asked real questions—about meaning, about people—before you ever asked about status." He paused again. "And that you were kind in ways that actually cost you something."

My chest felt tight in a good way, like something was loosening inside.

I looked down at my untouched burger, then back up at him. "I'm still figuring a lot of stuff out. About myself. About… everything."

His smile was small, almost private. "So am I."

That caught me off guard. "You?"

"Yeah." He lifted one shoulder. "Money fixes schedules and problems. It doesn't fix being alone. Or knowing what you're really here for. Or who you can actually trust when the room goes quiet."

Hailey's expression softened. Even Marcus stopped trying to crack jokes.

I nodded slowly. "Thanks for telling me that."

"Thanks for asking," he said.

Our hands brushed on the table—nothing dramatic, just fingers grazing for a second. Neither of us pulled away.

And for the first time since Starbucks, since the wink across the arena, since the tickets that still felt impossible…

It didn't feel like a mystery anymore.

It felt like the beginning of something real. Like permission to stop guessing and just… be.

We ate the burgers and fries, and drank the drinks. Glances were shared and it was a pleasant lunch. But it was far from over. The noise of the park faded again—not gone, just distant. Like the world was politely giving us space.

I stared at my hands for a second too long.

"There's one more thing," I said. "And I don't usually ask this kind of question because it makes me feel… small."

Gabriel didn't interrupt. Didn't reassure. He waited.

I looked up. "If I matter to you—if this is even a *possibility*—how do you keep someone like me from becoming… temporary?"

Hailey's breath caught. Marcus went very still.

I pushed through. "I don't mean emotionally. I mean realistically. Your life is… large. Mine is quieter. I don't want to be someone you enjoy and then outgrow."

Gabriel's expression changed—not wounded, not defensive.

Serious.

"That question doesn't make you small," he said. "It makes you precise."

He leaned forward slightly. "I don't keep people by outgrowing them. I keep them by choosing them—again and again—when novelty wears off."

"And when life gets messy?" I asked.

"Especially then."

I swallowed. "And if I can't always keep up?"

He shook his head. "I don't want someone who keeps up. I want someone who *walks beside me*—even if the pace changes."

Silence settled again.

Then—deliberately—Gabriel shifted.

"Can I ask you something now?" he said.

My stomach flipped. "Okay."

He held my gaze. "You talk about equality. About presence. About love that's built, not given." His voice was calm, but intent. "What happens when that kind of love asks something difficult of you?"

I frowned slightly. "Like what?"

"Like patience," he said. "Or trust. Or staying when walking away would feel safer."

I hesitated.

He didn't fill the space.

"I've left before," I admitted. "When I felt like I was becoming optional."

"And if you weren't?" he asked quietly.

I exhaled. "Then I'd have to learn not to run."

He nodded once, as if filing that away.

"One more," he said.

I managed a small smile. "You're not pulling any punches."

"Neither are you."

He softened. "What are you actually afraid I'll see in you… If I look too closely?"

That one hit.

I looked away, then back. "That I want something real more than I want to admit. And that I don't know how to protect it once I have it."

Gabriel's voice lowered. "Then we're standing in the same place."

Our hands found each other—this time on purpose.

And no one pulled away.

The sun began dipping low. The park lights came on. Kids got cranky. Parents looked like they needed strong beverages.

Hailey and Marcus rejoined us, both grinning like they'd witnessed a royal engagement.

"So," Hailey whispered as we walked to the car, "how was your *date*?"

"It wasn't a date."

"Nathan," she said, grabbing my shoulders, "you held hands on a roller coaster. That's a relationship milestone."

Marcus chimed in, "My parents didn't hold hands until after four years of marriage. You're basically engaged."

I shoved them toward the car.

Gabriel walked us to the parking lot but stopped short of the vehicle.

"I should go," he said softly.

"Yeah," I said, suddenly unable to look directly at him without my heart malfunctioning.

He hesitated.

Then— "Nathan… may I contact you?"

My breath caught. "Contact me?"

"As in… call. Text. Speak beyond chance encounters. Something real."

I nodded. "Yeah. I'd like that."

He smiled—slow, warm, hopeful. "Good. Let me see your phone so I can add my number."

Hailey and Marcus waved from the car windows like lunatics.

Gabriel walked away, disappearing into a soft glow of parking lot lights.

When I got in the car, Hailey screamed into a grocery bag.

Marcus clutched his Tweety like it was the Holy Grail.

"HE GAVE YOU HIS NUMBER!" Hailey shrieked.

My phone buzzed.

A new text from an unknown number:

Gabriel: *Thank you for today. I'd like to see you again — without roller coasters or cartoon interference. If you're willing.*

My heart lifted, weightless.

I typed back:

Me: *I'm willing.*

The car ride home was a blur of neon signs, half-screamed theories, and Hailey shaking my shoulders every time she remembered that Gabriel— billionaire, restaurateur, WWE sponsor, mystery man — wanted to see me again. I should've been floating for the next forty-eight hours, but the truth was simple: I didn't know what this meant. Not yet. Still, that night I fell asleep with my phone on my chest and a stupid smile on my face.

By Monday morning, the glow hadn't faded — but reality had quietly crept back in. Work was work. Scripts were scripts. Training was training. And even though I kept checking my phone like a teenager waiting for a crush to text back, the world around me went back to humming in its normal, predictable rhythm.

Until it didn't.

(9) The VP, the Rumor, & the Envelope

By week four of training, the initial buzz of the new job had settled into something almost cozy—like a roller coaster that's climbed the first big hill so many times the climb feels safe… right up until you remember what comes next.

The city no longer felt like it was staring me down. The building had started to carry my scent, not just everyone else's. Even the headset had stopped trying to crush my skull.

Then the rumor dropped.

It began as low murmurs by the coffee station: "A major executive is coming through on Friday. Touring the whole floor." "No one's saying who." "But it's someone big. Like, *really* big."

My stomach did a slow, nauseating flip.

Marcus, mouth full of sandwich, leaned across the table at lunch. "What if it's the CEO? I'm serious."

Hailey rolled her eyes. "CEOs don't slum it with trainees who still double-click hyperlinks. Come on."

"But they're saying he's young," Marcus pressed, eyebrows doing their annoying dance. "Young, loaded, stupidly handsome. Like…   could-walk-onto-a-soap-opera-and-steal-the-lead handsome. Controls divisions. Moves money around like it's chess. Personally scouts talent."

I stopped breathing for half a second.

No. Absolutely not. That was my brain taking one perfect afternoon—talking, laughing, the way Gabriel's eyes crinkled when he teased me on the ride—and pasting it onto corporate gossip like a bad Photoshop job.

I forced the bite down, chewed mechanically. *He wouldn't come here. He probably doesn't even set foot in buildings like this. He's… somewhere else. Important. Untouchable.*

By midweek the whispers had metastasized: "Nineteen percent stake in the parent company." "Quietly shifting assets between divisions." "He's reviewing trainee performance files himself." "Word is he likes to see potential in person."

Every new fragment landed like a heartbeat I couldn't quiet. My pulse thrummed in my ears during calls, during breaks, during the long silences when I stared at my screen and saw his face instead of spreadsheets.

Friday morning the air felt charged, electric. Even the printers seemed to hum with anxiety.

At 10:15 sharp, the announcement came: assemble on the training floor. All thirty of us. Lined up like recruits waiting for inspection.

This was it. The doors at the far end stayed closed a beat too long. My hands were clammy. My throat dry. I told myself it was ridiculous, impossible, but part of me—stupid, hopeful, still glowing from that afternoon—kept whispering: *What if.*

The doors opened.

And in walked…

Ralph Emerson.

I'd seen the photo in the new-hire packet. The same one smiling blandly from the digital billboard in the lobby a few weeks back. The guy on the billboard we'd passed on the highway. Here he was in person: middle-aged, with thinning dark hair combed carefully over a bald spot, a sensible navy suit, and the slight forward hunch of someone who'd spent too many years in ergonomic chairs that weren't quite ergonomic enough.

He looked exactly like a Vice President of Client Affairs should look: professional, forgettable, utterly devoid of mystery.

Not Gabriel. Not even in the same universe.

"Good morning, everyone," he said, voice smooth and measured, the kind that belonged in quarterly earnings calls or tax seminars. "I'm Ralph Emerson, Vice President of Client Affairs. I'm here today to observe your progress and answer any questions you might have about our client portfolio."

The room exhaled. I felt the air leave my lungs in a rush—half relief, half ridiculous disappointment.

Of course it was Ralph Emerson. Of course it wasn't 'him'.

Next to him stood a tall woman with impeccable eyeliner and a clipboard capable of killing small insects on impact.

"This is my executive secretary, Hilary," Mr. Emerson continued. "She is, frankly, more important than I am."

Hilary nodded once, confirming this fact.

The entire room seemed to deflate — a collective exhale of: "That's it? This is the powerful man we were terrified of?"

I forced myself not to laugh out loud. Of course it wasn't Gabriel. Of course the universe wasn't that on-the-nose.

Mr. Emerson gave a speech so dry it could've dehydrated fruit. Something about growth projections. Something about opportunity. Something about being "the future of the company."

He left as swiftly as he entered, as if allergic to being on lower floors.

We relaxed. We teased. We moved on.

Until lunch.

I'd just sat down with a microwaved lasagna when Hailey ran toward me like she'd seen the ghost of a cancelled paycheck.

"NATHAN!" she hissed. "You have a meeting."

"With who?" I asked, fork halfway to my mouth.

"Mr. Emerson."

My fork fell. "WHAT? Why?! What did I do?"

"No idea," she said breathlessly. "But Hilary came down personally. She said you are to report to the 24th floor by 4:30 PM. Alone."

I felt my stomach evacuate the premises.

Marcus joined us, wide-eyed. "Ohhhh no. Nathan. Buddy. Pal. You're dead. You committed a crime."

"I DID NOTHING!" I cried.

"That's what guilty people say!"

By the time I actually got into the elevator at 4:28 PM, my hands were shaking. I'd never been above floor 12. The numbers climbed painfully:

18… 19… 20…

"What does he want?" I whispered to myself.

21… 22… 23…

I didn't know Mr. Emerson. I'd never spoken to him. Why me?

The doors swished open.

The air changed. Carpet softer. Walls darker. Lights warmer. Everything expensive.

Hilary stood waiting for me like a tall, elegant gargoyle of professionalism.

"Nathan," she said briskly. "Follow me."

Her heels clicked with judgment as she escorted me into a corner office overlooking the city. The view made my building look like a Lego block.

Mr. Emerson stood at his desk.

"Nathan," he said, as if we were old colleagues. "Come in."

I stepped inside.

Hilary closed the door behind me — and left for the day.

Suddenly it was just the VP and me.

He gestured to a chair. "Sit."

I sat.

"Would you like something to drink?" he asked.

"No thank you," I squeaked.

He nodded, walked behind his desk, then stopped in front of a large framed photo of the building. He lifted it—revealing a sleek, concealed wall safe.

My stomach dropped into the Earth's mantle.

Oh God. Is this where he keeps the complaint files? Are they about to fire me? Is this where I get offered a settlement before being thrown into the street?

He opened the safe. Reached inside. Pulled out a padded envelope.

Turned.

And handed it to me.

"Nathan," he said calmly, "I was instructed to give you this."

My heart stopped.

"By who?" I whispered.

"That," he said, "I was not told. Only this: You are not to open the envelope until you are safely inside your apartment. Understood?"

"No." My voice cracked. "But… yes?"

"Good," he said, sitting down.

I stared at the envelope as if it were ticking.

"Is this… good news?" I asked cautiously.

Mr. Emerson shrugged. "It's… news. The nature of it is not my business. I was simply asked to deliver it — discreetly."

My palms were sweating. My heart pounded. My mind raced with every possible scenario, from job promotion to murder threat to Gabriel-related madness.

"You may leave," he said gently.

I stood slowly, bowed (for some reason — why?), grabbed the envelope, and walked out of the office with all the grace of a duck learning to roller-skate.

The elevator doors closed behind me, and I finally let out the breath I'd been holding for ten minutes.

What… the hell… was happening?

Who would send me something through a VP? Why all the secrecy? Why me?

And why did the smallest part of me whisper:

Gabriel.

But no — that wasn't possible. Was it?

The envelope felt heavy in my hands.

Mysterious. Warm. Dangerous. Hopeful.

Whatever was inside it…

…it was about to change something.

I just didn't know what.

(10) Envelope With My Name in Gold

The walk home felt longer than any walk I'd taken since moving to the city. My legs worked, but my mind was somewhere else entirely — looping, spinning, questioning every interaction I'd had in the last month.

Why me? What did I do? What did Mr. Emerson mean by "discreet"? Who delivered it? Who instructed it? What could POSSIBLY be inside?

I was so deep in thought that I didn't even hear Hailey and Marcus running up behind me.

What I *did* hear was a sudden, violent "BOO!" followed by two hands latching onto my ribs like claws.

I screamed. LOUD. I think a pigeon three blocks away died from the shockwave.

I also peed a little. Don't judge me.

The envelope nearly flew out of my hands.

"HAILEY!" I gasped, clutching my chest. "WHY. Why would you do that? Am I dying? Do I LOOK like I needed that?"

She giggled like a gremlin. "Your face, Nathan. Oh my God. Worth it."

Marcus appeared behind her with a container of Chinese noodles. "We brought dinner… and entertainment."

"Y-yeah," I said weakly, "you almost brought my soul straight to God."

Hailey noticed the envelope in my grip. "What's this?!"

I clutched it to my chest like a newborn infant. "I don't know, okay?! I was told not to open it until I got home."

"Sooo mysterious!" Marcus teased, elbowing me. "What happened? Why did the VP want you? Were you promoted? Fired? Sold to a traveling circus?"

"Marcus!" I snapped. "Keep your circus fantasies to yourself. And I'm not allowed to say anything yet."

They both groaned dramatically.

"You HAVE to tell us," Hailey pleaded. "Promise! We want ALL the tea. ALL OF IT. First-date-with-a-loverboy energy."

I rolled my eyes. "Maybe. Maybe not."

"Oooooh, he's being secretive," Marcus said, swirling his noodles like an evil mastermind. "I hate it. I love it."

When we reached our floor, they reluctantly peeled off toward their own apartments. I gave them a weak wave before closing my door behind me.

Instant silence.

I held the envelope as if it might explode.

I dropped my bag. Stripped off my sweaty shirt. Decided the moment needed a shower because my armpits smelled like fear and anxiety.

Ten minutes later, fresh clothes, damp hair, and my takeout in hand, I sat at the table.

The envelope stared at me. I stared back. It won the staring contest.

I paced in a circle while shoveling noodles into my face. I sat. I stood. I circled again. I took a long, dramatic sip of water. I tapped my teeth like a small rodent.

"What is this?" I asked the envelope, thinking it owed me an explanation.

Then the phone rang.

I screamed. Actual scream. I think my neighbors thought a murder was in progress.

It was Mom.

Of course.

I fumbled the phone open with trembling fingers. "Hi, Mom."

"Oh sweetheart, just checking in on my baby!"

"Mom, I'm twenty-five."

"To me you're five."

I sighed. We chatted for ten minutes — her updates, Dad's sermon going long, a lady from church getting engaged again, the dog misbehaving — the usual. I begged her (nicely) to let me go.

When the call ended, I placed the phone down and glared at the envelope again.

"Okay. No more delays."

I picked it up.

No stamps. No return address. No corporate print markings.

Just one thing:

My full name was embossed in gold. *Nathan Leigh Moffett.*

It looked elegant. Fancy. Beautiful, even.

What was wrong with me? Why was I admiring the font at a time like this? I was losing it.

I slid a finger under the flap— "AH— DAMN IT—"

Paper cut.

Of course.

I tended to it, muttering curses, then came back with disinfected vengeance.

I opened it carefully this time.

Slowly —

slowly —

as if the universe itself were holding its breath—

And then I tipped the contents onto the table.

Everything inside spilled out like a memory exploding before me.

I froze.

My heart stopped.

My world tilted.

Because in front of me were:

1. A photo of the Disney castle in Florida.

Bright, glowing, postcard-perfect.

2. A photo of me and my mother outside that same castle.

Arms around each other. I was obviously smiling too big. Her kissing my cheek. A moment frozen from a lifetime ago.

I gasped.

Then my eyes moved to—

3. A small, thin blue diary.

My diary. *My* diary from that Florida trip. My handwriting inside. My wishes all written with a child's shaky sincerity.

Wishes about:

— dressing as a Disney prince — marrying the man of my dreams in the castle — working at Disney one day — creating magic for other people because I never felt like I had enough of it

My throat tightened.

How did this diary get here? I hadn't seen it in years. I thought it was lost.

I reached out with trembling fingers.

The next item—

4. A photo of the black motorcycle I'd seen outside my building.

Clear. Crisp. Exactly the same bike. I swallowed hard. Then—

5. A key.

A flat, sleek, metal key. Cold in my hand. A motorcycle key? My pulse pounded in my ears. And finally—

6. A black card with gold lettering.

Minimalist. Heavy. Luxurious. On one side: An address.

On the other: Gabriel's Sogno Toscano — the most expensive Italian restaurant in the city. — the one critics call "untouchable." — the one with a year-long waitlist. — the one the wealthy whisper about.

Named after…Gabriel…I had forgotten to ask Gabriel the other day about the coincidence.

My breath shook.

I sat down slowly. The room spun.

This wasn't a coincidence. This wasn't random. This wasn't small.

Someone had:

— found my childhood diary — kept my childhood photo — linked me to the bike — known my mother — known my dreams — known *me*

Even the restaurant card…Sogno Toscano. Italian for: "Tuscany Dream" or "The Dreamer's Tuscany."

And Gabriel, the man I'd met and spent an afternoon getting to know on Sunday… the man I'd glimpsed numerous times… the man I hadn't stopped thinking about even today…

My heart whispered: *It's him.* My head whispered: *He's THE one I wished for all those years ago* My soul whispered: *Of course he is…he has to be.*

I looked at the diary again.

My childhood handwriting looked back.

A wish I'd whispered to a star.

And suddenly…

I wasn't sure if I wanted answers. Or if I was terrified of them.

(11) The Ball I Never Expected to Attend

I stood there in my quiet apartment, clutching the diary and photos to my chest like holy relics, staring at the key and the black card on the table as if they might spring to life and deliver an explanation.

Nothing happened.

My breath came in short, tight bursts. My eyes glazed over. I felt myself slip somewhere between excitement and terror — that dizzy, lightheaded place where the world spins but your feet don't move.

Then reality snapped back like a rubber band:

"Oh. My. God." I whispered. "I don't have anything to wear."

Of course THAT was my first concern. Not the diary from my childhood magically reappearing. Not the motorcycle photo. Not the key. Not the fact that the card said *Gabriel's Sogno Toscano,* the city's most elite Italian temple of wealth and food.

No. Clothes. My brain housed a fashion emergency first.

"Okay," I muttered, pacing. "Surely I have SOMETHING."

I tore into my closet like raccoons tear into trash — violently, with poor judgment. Within minutes, the bed was buried under an unholy mountain of shirts, pants, mismatched socks, jackets that still had tags on them, and a vest I bought once because a YouTube stylist lied to me.

"Oh no," I breathed. "I'm screwed. I'm Cinderella with no birds to sew me a damn suit."

That's when another realization struck:

"I DON'T KNOW WHEN I'M SUPPOSED TO GO!"

Panic detonated.

I bolted down the hallway so fast the carpet threatened to file a complaint. I reached Hailey's door and pounded like the FBI conducting a raid.

She opened it in curlers and pajamas, holding ice cream, and said, "What in the actual— NATHAN?!"

"HAILEY, I NEED YOU."

Her eyes bulged. She didn't ask another question. Instead, she dropped her ice cream, grabbed my wrist, and together we sprinted down the hall.

We pounded on Marcus's door like villagers demanding the monster. He opened half-asleep with headphones around his neck.

"What—why are—HEY—!"

We dragged him out before he could put on his shoes.

Back in my apartment, I dumped the contents of the envelope onto the table like a magician revealing a cursed trick.

Hailey gasped. Marcus swore. Twice.

"What the— whose— HOW?!" Hailey shrieked, picking up the restaurant card. "Nathan, WHAT IS THIS?"

"I HAVE NO IDEA!" I squealed.

Marcus held up the motorcycle key. "Bro. BRO. Did you buy a bike?! Did someone DIE and leave you their midlife crisis?"

"NO!"

"Then—WHAT IS HAPPENING?"

"I DON'T KNOW!"

They studied everything, mesmerized. But I didn't let them touch the diary. I held it protectively against my chest like a child clutching a stuffed animal.

"I… I have to go to this restaurant," I whispered, voice tiny. "But I don't know when."

Marcus flipped the card over. "It's right here."

"How did I miss that?!" I cried.

"Because you panic," Hailey said. "It's your charm."

I leaned in.

In the lower right corner, in tiny, elegant print:

Saturday, 7:00 PM.

"THAT'S TOMORROW!"

I spun around dramatically and pointed at my bed. "AND I HAVE NOTHING TO WEAR."

Hailey surveyed the clothing mountain with the grim resignation of a general reviewing fallen troops.

"Well," she said, "the mall closes in three hours. Let's go."

"I CAN'T TAKE THE BIKE!" I shouted as she grabbed the key.

"Why not?! You look like a biker virgin but I can teach you!"

"HAILEY, NO. The only thing dying tonight is my fashion sense, not ME."

We marched to the parking garage anyway and found the bike in spot **#24** — sleek, black, silently intimidating.

"The key's probably for the ignition," Marcus said.

"Nope," I said. "Already tried."

I looked around the bike, found the tiny storage compartment near the speedometer, inserted the key…

Click.

It opened.

Inside was another envelope.

I lifted it out, flipped it open…

…and screamed.

Inside was a $15,000 VISA gift card …in MY NAME. And a tiny note written in the neatest handwriting I'd ever seen:

Dress well.

I screamed again.

Hailey screamed because I screamed. Marcus screamed because Hailey screamed. The garage echoed with chaos.

We stumbled onto the street to breathe—and stopped.

A limo idled at the curb. A man in a suit stepped out and opened the door.

"For Mr. Moffett," he said politely. "To assist with his… preparations."

I swear my soul left my body.

We slid into the limo, still screaming internally. The driver handed us bottled water and asked where to.

"The mall!" Hailey barked. "Full emergency!"

Marcus nodded solemnly. "It's life or death."

I burrowed into the plush seats, clutching the 15K card like it was radioactive.

The mall had never looked so magical.

We spent thirty minutes debating stores. Do we go high fashion? Formalwear? Something bespoke? Do I dress like a CEO? A prince? A secret agent? A man going on a mysterious date with someone I couldn't admit I hoped it was?

Finally we found it:

BARTON & WELLS Formalwear — A luxury boutique so elegant it smelled rich.

The mannequins wore tuxedos that looked like they did taxes for fun. The walls were lined with fabrics I didn't know existed. A sales associate materialized out of nowhere, smiling the smile of someone who lives off commission.

"Gentlemen, ladies," he said, clapping his hands, "let's create magic."

I must've tried on twenty jackets. Ten shirts. Seven pairs of shoes.

We debated bowtie vs. regular tie for fifteen minutes while the associate nodded with professional patience.

We swiped fabric. Held up colors. Checked mirror angles. Compared cuts.

Hailey picked up a white cashmere scarf. Marcus held up a red bowtie. I put on a perfectly tailored black suit with satin lapels and…

Everything clicked.

Me, but elevated. Me, but mysterious. Me, but ready.

I looked… legit.

The associate tapped his chin. "We can do alterations by 3 PM tomorrow," he said. "You will look extraordinary."

I swallowed hard. "Do it."

We paid. The limo took us back. And as I stepped out, the driver gave a respectful nod:

"Sir, I will pick you up at 6:00 PM sharp."

I stood there in the night air, shaking.

Tomorrow. 7:00 PM. Gabriel's Sogno Toscano.

It was Gabriel. It had to be. The motorcycle was his, I'm partially sure from that one night he was on it at the street curb…and then it was parked in the garage with the gift card gleaming in the locked box. Knowing I couldn't handle the bike, he'd provided a surprise limo that showed up like something from a dream and the black card invitation etched in that precise, confident font. These weren't coincidences. They were breadcrumbs, and they'd led straight to him.

As I got started up to my apartment, I hugged the diary tighter, thumb brushing the worn cover where my clumsy kid-handwriting still peeked out. The photo—me, gap-toothed, grinning in front of that same damn castle on the postcard. These were *mine*. Not borrowed. Not gifted from a stranger's collection.

So how had they ended up in an envelope addressed to me, courtesy of a man I'd only just met?

My stomach twisted—equal parts thrill and unease.

Tomorrow I'd ask him. Straight out. No more games.

Or at least… I hoped I'd have the nerve.

(12) The Night Text Wouldn't Stop

By the time I got home, my feet hated me, my shoulders hated me, and my gift card was burning a hole in my pocket.

Clothes shopping with Hailey was like competing in an Olympic event nobody warned me about. Marcus, meanwhile, remained impressively chill—chill enough to vanish and return later with Dairy Queen blizzards like a man on a snack-based side quest.

I tossed the accessories garment bag over a chair, kicked off my shoes, and collapsed face-first onto the bed. I didn't bother turning off the lamp. I was too exhausted to care.

My phone buzzed beside me.

I groaned, rolled over, and checked the screen.

A text from Gabriel—my newest addition, one I now recognized by heartbeat alone.

Gabriel: *I hope you got the envelope I left for you… And I see you found the gift card.*

I blinked, then glanced at the dresser where the torn envelope and high-limit gift card sat like two small pieces of a much larger puzzle.

Of course he knew.

Me: *Were you watching me?*

Three dots appeared. Disappeared. Returned.

Gabriel: *Let's call it… verifying. I wanted to be sure you wouldn't miss it.*

I sat up, rubbing my eyes.

Me: *Gabriel, you didn't have to do that. I'm not used to people… preparing things for me.*

Gabriel: *I know. I could tell.*

His messages felt different tonight. Softer. Less composed. Like he'd peeled back a layer on purpose.

Me: *The gift card was too much. It felt—*

I hesitated.

Gabriel: *Intrusive?*

Me: *No. Just unexpected. In a good way. I think. It's just… no one's ever done something like that for me.*

A pause.

Gabriel: *Then I'm honored to be the first.*

My chest tightened.

Me: *Why? The envelope, the card, the reservation… all of it?*

His reply took longer this time.

Gabriel: *Because tomorrow matters to me. And because I wanted you to feel prepared, not panicked.*

Me: *Panicked?*

Gabriel: *You carry a lot alone, Nathan. Even more than you admit.*

That landed harder than I expected.

Me: *Have you really been paying that much attention?*

Gabriel: *Not watching. Learning.*

I exhaled. He had a way of softening the sharpest truths.

Me: *Well… I did use the gift card. Hailey made me try on half the store.*

Gabriel: *I know.*

I froze.

Me: *Were you there?*

Gabriel: *Not inside. Relax. I just wanted to be sure you weren't overwhelmed. You looked... determined. And tired. And wonderful.*

My face burned.

Me: *Gabriel—*

Gabriel: *I won't apologize for caring. If I ever overstep, tell me. I'll listen.*

Something settled in my chest—not dizzying, not overwhelming. Just steady.

Me: *You're not overstepping. Just... surprising me.*

Gabriel: *Then let me surprise you a little more. You looked incredible in that tuxedo.*

I glanced at the accessory garment bag.

Me: *Yeah.*

Gabriel: *Wear it tomorrow with pride. Don't forget the cufflinks, cummerbund, bowtie... and the pocket watch—everything is in the accessory bag.*

Me: *Pocket watch?*

Gabriel: *Check your bag.*

I laughed.

Me: *They're going to think I stole it.*

Gabriel: *No. I had someone slip it in. I wanted it to feel discovered, not delivered.*

That made me smile.

Me: *You're dangerous.*

A pause.

Gabriel: *The gold brings out the blue in your eyes.*

My breath caught.

Me: *You say things that make sleep difficult.*

Gabriel: *Then don't sleep yet. Tell me something true. Are you nervous about tomorrow?*

I didn't dodge it.

Me: *Yes. A lot.*

His reply came instantly.

Gabriel: *Me too.*

I blinked.

Me: *You?*

Gabriel: *I don't want to rush you. And I don't want tomorrow to be the last time I see you.*

The room felt very quiet.

Me: *It won't be.*

Gabriel: *Good. Rest now, Nathan. Tomorrow matters.*

Me: *Goodnight, Gabriel.*

Gabriel: *Goodnight. And Nathan?*

Me: *Yeah?*

Gabriel: *You're worth preparing for.*

I stared at the screen, thumb hovering. The question had been circling since I first opened that envelope, and tonight—after all this—I couldn't leave it hanging.

Me: *One more thing before I try to sleep. I'd like to ask you why you had my stuff from the past in the envelope. The photo of me as a kid, the Disney castle postcard, the diary... those were mine when I was little. How did you end up with them?*

The three dots appeared almost immediately. They stayed a long time.

Gabriel: *I've been thinking about how weird this all must seem, so I want to just lay it out plainly.*

A few years back I went to this local charity auction—mostly household stuff from estate sales and people downsizing. There was a small box of random personal items up for bid, nothing fancy, just old kid stuff like a diary, some photos, a couple little keepsakes. I ended up getting it cheap because no one else was really interested.

When I looked through it later, I saw your full name written inside the front cover of the diary in that careful kid handwriting, and one of the photos had your last name and a date scribbled on the back. It rang a faint bell—my aunt used to talk about our old neighborhood, the families, little stories from back then, and your name came up once or twice in that context. I figured it was probably you (or at least someone from the same circle), but I had no way to track anyone down at the time.

Honestly, I kept them because they felt… I don't know, innocent? Like a little time capsule from someone's better days. I stuck the box in a drawer and kind of forgot about it until I met you and things started clicking. Same name, same area growing up, same age range—it hit me that it really was yours.

I didn't say anything sooner because I didn't want it to feel like some creepy setup or like I was holding onto them for leverage. That was never it. They just didn't belong with me. So when the moment felt right, I wanted to give them back properly. I'm sorry I let the mystery drag on—I should've just come out with it from the start. Just wanted you to know the real story.

My eyes stung a little. Not from suspicion anymore—from relief. From the quiet sweetness of it.

Me: *That's… actually kind of beautiful. Thank you for keeping them safe. And for giving them back.*

Gabriel: *You're welcome. No more secrets between us tonight. Sleep now. I'll see you tomorrow.*

I set the phone down, screen dark. The diary still sat on the dresser, but it didn't feel borrowed anymore. It felt returned. Tomorrow wasn't about questions. It was about us.

Gabriel's POV — The Night Before the Date

He should have been asleep.

The city was winding down—assistants, chefs, night managers, all executing their closing rituals. His world functioned on systems.

But Gabriel sat in his study, phone in hand, rereading Nathan's last messages: *That's… actually kind of beautiful. Thank you for keeping them safe. And for giving them back.*

He exhaled, long and slow. The truth had been simple all along—no hidden connections, no elaborate schemes. Just a box from a charity auction years ago, a name that stuck in his memory, and a decision to hold onto something small and hopeful until the right moment arrived.

He shouldn't have texted first tonight. Shouldn't have needed to hear Nathan say thank you. Shouldn't have felt this much relief at being believed.

Wanting had never frightened him before. Until now.

When Nathan asked about the envelope, Gabriel had braced for doubt, for distance. Instead came gratitude. Acceptance. Something inside him loosened—not painfully, but honestly.

People prepared meetings with him on a constant basis. Nathan had never been one of those people. That was exactly why he mattered.

Tonight, for the first time in years, the loneliness felt smaller. Not gone—just… quieter.

He reread Nathan's words one last time, then set the phone facedown. Tomorrow mattered. And for once, Gabriel Michaels believed tomorrow could be the beginning of something that lasted.

(13) The Things He Learned to Carry

Gabriel learned early that love was conditional.

Not because his parents withheld it entirely—but because it was *measured*. Apportioned. Rewarded for achievement, withheld for weakness. In his family, affection followed excellence the way applause follows performance.

He grew up in a country that prized discipline and appearances, where reputation mattered more than comfort and legacy mattered more than joy. His father believed in order. His mother believed in composure. Both believed in sacrifice—especially their own, which they reminded him of often.

"You will have everything," his father once told him, voice calm and absolute. "But you will earn it first."

Gabriel was not an unhappy child.

That distinction mattered to him.

He had food. Tutors. Structure. Opportunity. But childhood, as other people described it—carefree, loud, indulgent—was not something he recognized when he later heard it discussed. He learned responsibility before pleasure. Precision before curiosity. Silence before expression.

He learned how to stand still while adults talked over him. How to listen without interrupting. How to swallow disappointment without showing it.

What he didn't learn—what no one taught him—was how to *rest*.

As a boy, Gabriel suspected something about himself that he did not yet have language for. It arrived quietly, not as shame but as *difference*. The way his attention lingered. The way admiration carried heat. The way certain friendships felt weighted with longing rather than rivalry.

He did not panic.

He compartmentalized.

Feelings, he decided, were information. They could be acknowledged privately and managed carefully. This philosophy served him well—for a long time.

By the time he reached university, Gabriel had already experienced his first failure.

Not publicly. Not dramatically. But internally.

He had loved once—briefly, intensely, and disastrously. A relationship conducted in shadows and hallways, defined by stolen moments and unspoken limits. When it ended, not from cruelty but fear, Gabriel learned another rule:

If something can be taken from you, do not build your life around it.

So he redirected.

Ambition was safer than intimacy. Achievement was more reliable than people. Control was kinder than hope.

Setbacks came—business risks that nearly ruined him, partnerships that dissolved overnight, men who saw his power before they saw *him*. He survived them all the way he survived everything: by adapting faster than anyone expected.

What the world saw was success.

What it did not see were the nights he sat alone in penthouses too quiet for their size. The meals were eaten across from people who admired him but never *knew* him. The way he sometimes stood at windows, watching the city live lives he could only pay for but not enter into himself.

He told himself this was the cost.

And for years, that was enough.

Until Nathan.

Nathan did not arrive like a disruption. He arrived like a question Gabriel had stopped asking.

Nathan didn't want anything from him—not access, not advantage, not security. He didn't perform. He didn't posture. He didn't pretend to be afraid.

That terrified Gabriel more than any negotiation ever had.

Because Nathan reminded him of the boy he once was—the one who learned to carry everything quietly, who learned to be competent instead of held, who learned to deserve love rather than expect it.

There were things Gabriel would not tell Nathan yet.

Not about the nights he'd convinced himself loneliness was a reasonable trade. Not about the relationship that taught him restraint at the cost of joy. Not about the moments he nearly walked away from everything because it felt hollow.

Those truths would come later. Carefully. When trust had roots.

But there were things he *hoped* to tell him one day.

That he did not want to be admired anymore—only understood. That he wanted a life that included laughter without an agenda. That he dreamed, quietly, of building something that wasn't measured in numbers or headlines.

That his greatest fear wasn't failure.

It was choosing safety again when something real finally stood in front of him.

Tonight, standing alone in the dim light of his study, Gabriel allowed himself a dangerous thought:

Maybe his life had not been preparation for power. Maybe it had been preparation for *connection*.

He didn't know yet how much of himself he would give Nathan.

But for the first time, he wanted to find out.

And that— more than wealth, more than control, more than legacy— felt like hope.

Gabriel was nine the first time he learned the difference between praise and approval.

The house was unusually still that afternoon, the kind of quiet that meant something important was happening. He stood outside his father's study, fingers smoothing the crease of his jacket, rehearsing what he would say. In his hands was a folder—thin, immaculate—holding the results of an examination he had worked months to prepare for.

Top marks. Highest in his year.

The door opened without ceremony.

His father sat behind the desk, posture perfect, glasses already on as if he'd been expecting this interruption. Gabriel stepped forward and placed the folder neatly in front of him.

"I did well," he said—not proudly, not timidly. Just factual.

His father opened the folder, scanned the results, and nodded once.

"Good," he said.

Just that.

Gabriel waited.

Seconds passed. Then a minute. His mother, seated near the window with a cup of tea cooling untouched in her hands, smiled politely at him but said nothing.

"Well done," she added eventually, voice soft, controlled. "This is what we expect."

Expectation.

Not celebration. Not delight. Not the kind of warmth Gabriel had seen in other parents at school events—arms thrown around shoulders, laughter spilling freely.

His father closed the folder and slid it back across the desk.

"Consistency is what matters," he said. "Anyone can succeed once."

Gabriel nodded. He had learned to nod early.

As he turned to leave, his father spoke again—not unkindly, but decisively.

"You'll understand one day," he said. "Affection without standards makes weak men."

Gabriel paused at the door.

He wanted to ask a question then. Something small. Something dangerous.

What happens when you meet the standard? When are you allowed to rest?

But he didn't ask.

He walked back to his room, closed the door quietly, and placed the folder in a drawer instead of on the shelf. He lay on his bed, staring at the ceiling, feeling something settle inside him—not anger, not sadness exactly, but understanding.

Achievement brought safety. Composure brought peace. Need brought disappointment.

That night, when his parents passed his room, they did not stop. They assumed he was fine.

And Gabriel decided, very calmly, very clearly:

If approval had to be earned, then he would earn it endlessly. If affection were conditional, then he would never ask for it again.

He became excellent after that.

Not because he wanted praise— But only because excellence was quieter than longing.

(14) Arrival at the Dream

If excitement were heat, then I was a full-grown dragon. Not a cute baby dragon. Not a "toothless, misunderstood creature." No. A medieval, fire-breathing, scorched-earth dragon, ready to accidentally burn down the neighborhood with a sneeze.

The morning of the big night, I woke up with a single thought:

I am not worthy.

The second thought was:

MY ARMPITS ARE SWEATING LIKE THEY'RE AUDITIONING FOR A ROLE IN NIAGARA FALLS.

I ripped the covers off, paced the floor, threw myself on the bed, paced again, and then decided—by irrational instinct—that I *needed* to check on my formalwear one more time.

Just in case the suit spontaneously combusted overnight. Or turned ugly. Or the bowtie fled the country.

Unable to trust my own sanity, I grabbed a taxi and beelined to Barton & Wells with my receipt clenched in my fist. The sales associates took one look at me — disheveled, in jeans, sweating like a busted hydrant — and their faces twisted in suspicion.

Oh, the judgment. The micro-expression of: *Did you steal that receipt from Prince Charming himself, you thrift-store gremlin?*

I wanted to say: "Yes, it's STILL me, peasants. Yesterday I was a prince. Today I'm a potato. Life is complicated."

But instead, I stood my ground with pride.

And when they returned with *MY* suit, wrapped in silk garment bags and smelling of wealth, I swung it over my shoulder and strutted out like Beyoncé exiting a private yacht.

The confidence lasted exactly six minutes.

That's when I got home and discovered…

The air conditioner was dead.

Not weak. Not struggling. DEAD. Gone to Jesus. Ascended.

Heat smothered my apartment like a punishment from the Old Testament. I showered. Immediately sweated through. Showered again. Sweated again.

By shower number three, I was delirious.

I powdered my chest. Deodorized my soul. Drowned myself in cologne. Nothing worked.

I stared at myself in the mirror, hair damp, shirt sticking, lips trembling.

"…I can't do this."

I reached for my phone to cancel everything and go get chicken wings by the hotel pool next door. Just me, greasy fingers, and anonymity.

But then:

BAM BAM BAM!

Hailey burst in like a fairy godmother with curlers instead of wings.

"Oh NO you don't," she declared, grabbing my chin. "You are NOT ditching destiny because your AC took a personal day."

Marcus followed with a fan and a towel, dabbing my forehead like I was a boxer before a title match.

"You got this, bro. You look mysterious. And expensive. And sweaty, but we're working on that."

Between Hailey fixing every minute flaw and Marcus preventing me from melting into a puddle, somehow — SOMEHOW — I became a person again.

A handsome one. A mysterious one. A "my life is changing tonight" one.

By 5:58 PM, I stood in my perfect black suit, white scarf draped just so, red bowtie crisp and sharp, shoes gleaming like polished obsidian.

I looked ready.

But internally?

I was a casserole of terror.

The limo arrived at 6:00 PM sharp.

I stepped in.

Silence.

Just me and the driver, who probably had diplomatic immunity based on his posture alone.

Then I discovered the Bluetooth connection. A mistake. Or destiny.

Suddenly, the limo's acoustics flared with Mariah Carey, and my nerves melted. Shawn Mendes came next. Then Bieber. Then some club-style bass so heavy the rearview mirror vibrated.

I was in the vibe. I was the vibe. I was practically a music video.

Time blurred in the air-conditioned sanctuary. I felt my confidence rise, settle, pulse.

Then the limo slowed.

Right as Tone Loc started: "Let's do this…"

The door swung open.

The chauffeur gave a perfect bow and said, "I will remain here for your return, sir."

I tried to sneak him a twenty.

He didn't even blink. Just gently closed my hand around it and shut the door with professional finality.

I exhaled.

And turned—

—into a dream.

The building rose before me like a cathedral of warm marble and soft gold lighting. This wasn't a restaurant. This was a temple.

Gabriel's Sogno Toscano. Three Michelin stars. The kind of place celebrities whispered about and normal people pointed at from across the street.

And I, Nathan Leigh Moffett, child of a minister in a conservative small town, boy who once wished for a legacy, man who still doubted his worth…

…stood there in a suit tailored for destiny.

A diary in my heart. A mystery in my pocket. And an invitation I still couldn't comprehend.

I took one breath. Held it.

Then stepped toward the entrance.

Whatever tonight was — Whatever waited inside —my life was no longer small. No longer invisible. No longer quiet.

Tonight, something was beginning.

And Gabriel — whoever he truly was —was the reason.

(15) The Seat Meant for Him

The doors to Gabriel's Sogno Toscano opened like they were powered by angels and hydraulics. Warm light washed over marble floors. Soft violin music drifted through the foyer. The air smelled of truffle, rosemary, and money — real, generational money.

I swallowed.

A host appeared instantly, as if summoned by my panic alone.

"Good evening, Mr. Moffett," she said. She knew my name. Butterflies detonated in my stomach.

"This way, please."

No check-in. No searching the reservation list. No small talk.

Just immediate knowing.

She led me down a hallway draped in hanging silk and dim golden light. The walls shimmered slightly, like candlelight dancing on water. We stopped at a thick, floor-to-ceiling curtain made from a fabric so heavy it could double as armor.

She smiled, bowed, and pulled it aside.

Inside was a private dining room.

Private wasn't even the word — it was separate from reality. A table for two. Crystal glasses. A wine decanter carved from hand-blown obsidian glass. Roses in a low vase. Soft candlelight flickering off gold-edged china.

The atmosphere was so perfect it felt unreal.

Then the curtain fell shut behind me with a soft *whoosh*, sealing me off completely.

Silence.

Then, all at once —

My body chilled.

Not from temperature. Not from air conditioning.

From nerves so sharp they almost vibrated.

My heart hammered. My hands tingled. My back felt cold, but my face burned.

I shivered so abruptly the server at the corner took a concerned step forward.

"I'm fine," I said quickly. "It's not the temperature. It's just… nerves."

He nodded politely. "Would you like some water?"

"Yes, please. And, um… can I have iced tea?"

He blinked. A slow, incredulous blink.

At a three-Michelin-starred temple of cuisine, where the cheapest drink was a $65 wine pairing, I had just asked for iced tea.

"As you wish," he said, bowing.

I whispered, "Yeah… I do wish it."

When he left, the silence cocooned around me again. Thick. Still. Unnatural.

I couldn't hear a sound outside the curtain. No footsteps. No clatter. No voices.

It was like being inside a velvet dream.

I sat. I breathed. I waited.

Minutes passed.

Then more.

Then more.

My thoughts spiraled:

Did he forget? Did something happen? Did he change his mind? Is he here? Am I early? Did I pick the wrong suit? No — impossible — I look GOOD. Not good. Dangerously good.

My foot bounced under the table. I swayed to the faint hum of Jason Aldean pouring through my jittery head:

"Tonight looks good on you…"

I mouthed the last line, trying to ease the pressure in my chest.

And then—

FWHIPP—

The curtain snapped open with a bright flash of motion.

I jumped so hard I nearly knocked over the water glass.

But instead of a handsome, mysterious, beautiful man with a half-smile and secrets in his eyes…

In stepped the restaurant manager.

A handsome man, yes — but not *my* mystery.

"Señor Nathan," he said gently, his voice warm with apology, "I am very sorry for the disappointment."

"Disappointment?" I repeated, heart collapsing like a deflated air mattress.

He stepped closer.

"Your dinner guest regrets that he could not be here tonight. An emergency arose that required his immediate attention."

My throat tightened.

"He sends his deepest apologies," the manager continued softly. "And a promise to make it up to you very soon."

I swallowed the disappointment, hard and bitter.

"Oh," I whispered. "Okay. I… understand."

But did I? No. Not really.

The manager placed a hand over his heart in a respectful gesture.

"He hopes you will stay. He selected the full course for you and your… alternate dinner guest."

"Alternate?" I frowned.

"Yes, but he wishes the surprise to be intact. If it pleases you, I will send him in."

"Him?"

The manager smiled. "A very special friend. One he knew would soften the disappointment."

A sudden knock on the wooden panel just outside the second curtain behind me.

A deep, unmistakable voice called:

"Nathan? They said you're inside?"

I froze.

No. No way. That's impossible—

The manager opened the second curtain with a dramatic flourish.

And there he was.

Goldberg. THE Goldberg. My childhood hero, looking at me like we were long-lost cousins catching up at a reunion.

He smiled. "Hey, man. I heard you were expecting someone else. Hope I'm a decent replacement."

My soul left my body, filed for divorce, and ascended into the sky.

I attempted words. None worked.

He laughed, clapped a hand on my shoulder, and took the seat across from me — the seat that was supposed to be Gabriel's.

The manager placed a hand over his heart. "Señor Gabriel sends his regrets."

Just Gabriel. No last name.

But hearing it spoken in this sacred, elegant place…it hit differently.

The curtain closed behind the manager. Leaving me with:

A legend. A feast. A now filled chair I wish wasn't filled with someone other than Gabriel. And a swirl of emotions I couldn't pin down.

I smiled. I let myself relax. I let myself *try* to enjoy the night.

But inside…

I was crestfallen, no longer hopeful but confused.

And more curious than ever.

Because the seat across from me — the seat Goldberg now filled — wasn't just missing someone.

It was holding a promise.

That Gabriel wasn't done.

Not even close.

Goldberg watched Nathan from across the table.

The kid was trying. Trying to smile. Trying to be present. Trying to pretend the absence didn't matter.

But it mattered. A lot.

He saw the flickers:

The way Nathan's eyes kept drifting to the curtain. The way his shoulders slumped before he caught himself. The half-smile that didn't reach his eyes.

Goldberg had met thousands of fans. Thousands of people. Thousands of men looked at him with excitement.

But the way Nathan looked toward that curtain?

That was something else.

"Kid's already gone for him," Goldberg thought, taking a sip of wine.

He knew Gabriel. He knew what the man hid behind the polished smile and measured voice.

He knew the loneliness. He knew the fears. He knew the stakes.

And he knew one painful, simple truth:

Gabriel hadn't skipped this dinner. He'd been forced to.

Between the remodel plans — the one tailored specifically for Nathan — and the security threats that appeared out of nowhere, Gabriel had been backed into a corner.

He'd called Goldberg personally.

"Bill," Gabriel had said, voice tight, "Please. Go. He can't be alone."

Goldberg had never heard him sound like that.

Never.

So he came.

He watched Nathan push through disappointment with grace. He watched him laugh at stories, even though the ache never left his eyes. He watched him thank the servers, even though he was hurting.

And Goldberg, seasoned fighter, felt a tug of protectiveness he hadn't expected.

"This kid," Goldberg thought, "has no damn idea what's being done behind the scenes for him."

But he would.

Soon.

Goldberg hugged me before he left — a full, solid, bone-cracking, soul-shaking bear hug that realigned my skeleton and my emotions in one go. Then he climbed into his Hummer like it weighed nothing and drove off into the night.

A limo pulled up behind him.

The chauffeur opened the door with the same gentle professionalism he'd offered earlier.

"Thank you," I whispered as I climbed in.

The door clicked shut.

Silence wrapped around me like a blanket that was somehow too soft and too heavy at the same time. Even the little click-clacks of my thumbs typing a message to Gabriel felt muted.

Gabriel's phone vibrated in the back of the armored SUV.

Nathan's message:

Dinner was nice. Thank you for arranging it... I hope everything's okay.

Gabriel shut his eyes.

Nathan didn't deserve to be abandoned. Not tonight.

For forty-eight hours, everything had gone wrong.

The remodel — the private gesture meant to surprise Nathan — was spiraling:

Wrong materials. Structural issues. Contractors arguing. Designers panicking. Timelines collapsing.

He'd spent the entire day fighting fires to keep the project intact for Nathan's sake.

And ironically, the truth was:

"Project Overhaul" was nearly finished as Nathan was leaving the restaurant.

But before Gabriel could even breathe—

Crisis #2 hit.

His Head of Security burst into the war-room meeting.

"Sir, chatter on several channels. Possible tail on your vehicle. You are NOT entering a predictable location tonight. You cannot attend the dinner."

Gabriel's jaw clenched so tightly it hurt.

He argued. Negotiated. Tried to override protocol.

But the team wouldn't budge.

They saw risk.

He saw a man waiting for him in a stunning black tuxedo he'd suggested.

And when he realized he could not get to Nathan safely, he gave the only order he could live with:

"Send Goldberg."

Not as protection.

As comfort.

As a stand-in for the warmth Gabriel wanted to give in person.

Now, riding through the night in the back of an armored SUV, Gabriel stared at his reflection in the tinted glass — eyes exhausted, suit rumpled, regret carved in every line.

"I didn't want to miss it," he whispered.

The dinner. The moment Nathan walked in. The look on his face. Everything.

He wanted to apologize. He wanted to explain. He wanted to confess everything.

But he couldn't. Not yet.

The world he lived in — the danger, the power, the secrets — would swallow Nathan whole if Gabriel opened the door too quickly.

So he typed the safe lie:

Everything is okay. I'll explain soon.

And when he hit send, something inside him cracked.

For the first time in years…he wished he were just a normal man with a normal life and the freedom to show up for the person he wanted most.

The drive home was eerie in its stillness — muted city lights sliding by the windows, music off, only the hum of the engine filling the space.

I folded my hands together, staring at them in the reflection of the window.

I wasn't crying. Not exactly.

But something inside me had cracked — fragile, human, bruised.

The chauffeur kept glancing at me in the mirror.

"Are you alright, sir? Not to intrude… but you look very emotional. May I do anything for you?"

The kindness nearly undid me.

"No. I'm fine. Really." A shaky breath. "But… thank you for asking."

He nodded. "Of course."

Silence again — but this time gentler.

When the limo rolled to a stop in front of my building, I blinked.

Three large vans were parked at the curb:

Louis' Air Conditioning Experts West Elm Furniture Dreamline Bathrooms Done Right

Men moved quickly, finishing paperwork, packing tools, and loading equipment.

It looked like the finale of a home makeover show.

"What… in the… world?" I whispered.

The chauffeur opened my door.

"Have a good evening, Mr. Moffett."

I stepped onto the pavement slowly, staring as the vans pulled away into the night.

Louis' Air Conditioning Experts West Elm Furniture Dreamline Bathrooms Done Right

All of them disappeared around the corner. I'd seen an advertisement billboard for Dreamline.

I'd been gone three hours.

Three.

What happened?

The elevator ride to my floor felt like moving into someone else's story.

When I stepped into the hallway, Hailey burst out of her apartment like a raccoon caught rummaging in a pantry.

"Oh my GOD, you're back!" she shrieked. "You are NEVER going to believe what happened in your apartment!"

My heart dropped.

"Oh shit. Did it burn down?"

She doubled over laughing. "No! But NATHAN. Just—GO LOOK."

I edged past her, each step heavier than the last.

I opened my door.

And froze. Literally, I froze. The air conditioning blasted arctic air and I closed my eyes and relished in it. I was truly in heaven.

My apartment was…new.

Not cleaned. Not updated. Transformed. Marcus stood in the bathroom doorway taking pictures like a proud dad.

"DUDE! Remember that billboard?" he said breathlessly. "They did it. Whoever your mystery sugar— I MEAN GUY—is, holy crap. He got them to do it faster than anything I've ever seen."

I stared at my bathroom:

Steam shower. Rainfall fixtures. Marble counters. Backlit mirrors. Heated towel rack. Everything brand-new and gleaming.

Marcus said something about the curing time. I heard none of it.

Hailey tugged my arm. "Oh honey. Come look at the CLOSET."

The closet was…Velvet-lined. LED-lit. Custom. Beautiful.

In the master room, a king-sized bed. Perfect bedding. Everything looked soft and intentional and impossibly luxurious.

"Oh my God," I whispered. "Who… would even…?"

Marcus lowered his phone. "Nathan. Seriously. Who IS this guy? A politician? Movie star? Mafia heir? Undercover prince?? WHAT?!"

"I don't know," I managed. "I truly don't."

Hailey collapsed onto the bed dramatically. "Well, whoever he is, the boy has TASTE."

I exhaled shakily.

"Sit down," I said. "Both of you. I have to tell you everything."

Hailey squealed. Marcus grabbed popcorn.

I sat at the table.

The envelope. The gift card. The bike key. The diary pressed against my chest.

I looked at my friends — my anchors.

And said:

"Okay. Pull up a chair. Because tonight was unbelievable."

And I told them everything.

Everything except my diary.

That stayed pressed against my heart — too sacred, too personal, too true to share.

---

(16) Mr. Caller Please

Hailey was halfway through reenacting my facial expression when I first saw the steam shower ("—and then your lip did this little *quiver*, like a baby deer in a Disney movie—") when my phone buzzed.

I froze.

Gabriel appeared on the screen.

My pulse skyrocketed.

Hailey yelped and dove behind my bed like a soldier taking cover. Marcus jumped and spilled popcorn everywhere.

I opened the message.

Gabriel: *I heard the teams finished a little ahead of schedule. I hope everything is to your liking.*

I stared. My hands shook. My throat tightened.

Hailey whisper-screamed from her hiding spot, "TEXT HIM BACK! TEXT HIM BACK, YOU LOVESICK DEMIGOD!"

I glared at her, then typed carefully:

Me: *It's… incredible. I don't know what to say. Or how you managed this. Thank you!*

Three dots appeared.

Then disappeared. Then came back. Then disappeared again.

Before I could guess his next move—

My phone rang.

Hailey shrieked like she'd been shot. Marcus leapt onto the bed with a muffled "OH MY GOD." I stared at the screen, numb.

GABRIEL is calling…

My stomach dropped, flipped, did a cartwheel, then filed for disability.

I answered.

"Hello?" My voice cracked like a middle-school choir soloist.

And then— his voice.

Warm. Low. Softened at the edges, like he was smiling.

"Hi, Nathan. You're most welcome."

Everything in me melted.

"I—hi," I said, because apparently that's all my brain cells could manage.

A quiet exhale came through the line. "Before anything else… I needed to hear your voice."

My knees went weak. I sat down on the edge of my new bed because the floor was becoming unreliable.

"Did I—did I wake you?" he asked gently.

"No, no. I'm awake. I'm… very awake."

A soft laugh. "Good."

He hesitated.

Not awkwardly. Not nervously.

Thoughtfully. Like he was choosing each word.

"I wanted to ask you personally," he said, "How do you like everything?"

I pressed a hand against my chest to keep my heart from falling out.

"Gabriel…" I breathed. "It's—there aren't words. I don't understand how any of this even happened. I left for dinner and came back to… a completely different home."

On the other end of the line, he inhaled. Not smug. Not proud.

Emotional.

"I'm glad," he said softly. "I wanted it to feel like the place you deserved."

I swallowed hard.

"You didn't have to—"

"I know," he said immediately. "I didn't do it because I had to."

There was a quiet, vulnerable pause.

"I did it because… I wanted to take care of you. Even if only in small ways."

My vision blurred for a second.

Behind me, Hailey gasped into a pillow. Marcus mouthed OH MY GOD repeatedly like a broken robot.

I tried to form a coherent sentence. Managed half of one.

"You… you barely know me."

Another soft, warm exhale.

"Nathan," he said, "I know more than you think. Not in an invasive way. Just… the way a man pays attention when something about someone feels important."

My breath caught.

He lowered his voice.

"And I hope… You don't hate what I did tonight."

"Hate it?" I whispered. "Gabriel, it was… unbelievable."

Relief washed through his exhale.

"Good," he murmured. "I was worried."

"You? Worried?" I laughed shakily. "You're a billionaire who sponsors WWE. You own restaurants and skyscrapers. What could *you* possibly be worried about?"

A beat.

His voice dropped.

"Disappointing you."

Everything inside me went still.

Completely, utterly still.

I didn't know what to say. I didn't even know what to *feel*. I just… felt everything at once.

So I whispered the only truth I had:

"You didn't."

He breathed out like he'd been holding that air for years.

"Nathan… thank you."

Then his tone shifted — warm, hopeful, careful. "If you're willing," he said softly, "I'd like to see you again. Properly. No emergencies. No interruptions. Just you and me."

My heart leapt into my throat.

"I'm willing," I whispered.

And Gabriel answered in a way that made my entire soul light up: "Good. Then let's make this right."

I inhaled to respond—but suddenly Hailey and Marcus were in front of me, *competing* to see who could make the most deranged face. Cheeks puffed. Eyes crossed. Tongues out. It looked like two toddlers on a sugar rush.

I covered the receiver. "Hold on, Gabriel… let me put you on hold for a second. Two literal kindergarteners need to be escorted out of my room so the adults can talk."

I muted the call, grabbed both by their ears—not hard, just enough to remind them I had seniority—and guided them toward the door.

They protested dramatically, as if I were evicting them during a snowstorm.

Hailey threw her hands up. "Fine! But remember—no bathroom visits for you for like, two days. If you gotta tinkle, don't sprinkle. Come *visit*." She punctuated it with a wiggle.

Marcus spun in a circle like a chaotic peacock. "Tell Daddy I said goodnight and kisses!"

I nearly yeeted him down the hallway.

But Gabriel was still on the line.

So I shoved them both out, shut the door, exhaled a prayer for patience… and unmuted the call, ready to return to the dangerously attractive man waiting on the other end of the line.

I sank onto my new velvet-lined bed, still breathless from kicking my two gremlin-children-friends out of the room. I unmuted.

"Sorry about that," I said. "They're… feral."

Gabriel laughed softly. "I gathered. They care about you."

"They care about embarrassing me."

"That too," he admitted.

A comfortable silence stretched — warm, anticipatory.

Then: "Nathan," he said gently, "can I ask you something?"

"Of course."

"Are you… happy? With everything I arranged? The dinner, the… changes to your apartment?" His voice dipped, hesitant, vulnerable in a way I hadn't heard before. "I didn't want to overwhelm you."

I smiled instinctively. "No, Gabriel. I'm overwhelmed in the best way. But since we're being honest…"

I shifted on the bed, heart fluttering. "Can *I* ask *you* something?"

"Anything." And God — he meant it.

"Before we meet properly… I think it would help me to know who I'm walking toward. Just… little things. So I don't sit across from a stranger."

A quiet inhale from his end.

"Then ask," he said.

So I did.

"Where's home for you?"

A low hum, thoughtful. "I was born in Tuscany. My family moved a lot — Europe, Asia, the Middle East. My mother wanted me to be well-rounded. My father wanted me disciplined."

"Which one won?"

"They both did," he said with a faint smile in his voice. "I'm very… rounded and very disciplined."

I laughed. "Okay. Fair enough."

Next question: "What's something you genuinely love doing when you're not running empires?"

A pause. "Cooking," he said. "Real cooking. Bare hands, chopping board, nothing fancy. It grounds me."

I blinked in surprise. "You? In a kitchen? I figured you only supervised kitchens."

He chuckled. "Believe it or not, I'm very comfortable with a knife."

"Should that reassure me?"

"That depends," he teased softly, "on how our next dinner goes."

My face heated instantly.

I swallowed. "What's one goal you haven't reached yet?"

Another long pause.

"I want to build something lasting," he said. "Not buildings. Not businesses. Something… generational. Something that makes the world better after I leave it."

It was unexpectedly earnest. Unexpectedly hopeful.

I whispered, "That's beautiful."

"It's necessary," he murmured.

Then the conversation shifted. Intensified. Softened.

"Nathan?"

"Yeah?"

"Thank you," he said quietly. "For… asking me these things. Most people want to know my net worth. My properties. My power. You asked about my dreams."

I felt a tug in my chest.

"Well… that's because I'm not dating your wallet."

Silence.

Then a soft, stunned laugh — like I'd hit him in the chest.

"I wasn't aware we were already using the word dating," he said, voice warm.

I choked on air.

"I—I didn't mean—"

"I know," he whispered. "But I liked hearing it."

My heart was a mess of fireworks.

Then I asked the question. The one that hit him somewhere raw.

"Gabriel," I said slowly, "what do you want most in a partner? What do you need from someone so you don't feel alone in the world?"

Silence. Actual silence. Gabriel never hesitated. Never stumbled. Never lost footing.

But now? His breath caught.

"Nathan," he said quietly, almost reverently, "you have no idea how rarely anyone asks me that."

"I'm asking."

And that undid him. His voice changed — softened, cracked.

"I want someone honest," he whispered. "Someone who isn't afraid to look me in the eye and tell me the truth, even when it's hard. Someone who doesn't want my money or my influence —

someone who sees me when I walk into a room, not the things attached to me."

He exhaled shakily.

"And… someone who lets me love them fully. No suspicion. No fear. No… pretending."

My throat tightened.

"Gabriel," I said softly, "that's… that's real. That's good."

"It's all I've ever wanted," he murmured.

Then, barely audible:

"And I'm terrified of wanting it."

I breathed in deeply. Bracing myself. Because it was my turn.

"Do you remember what *I* look for?" I asked.

"Yes," he said instantly. "A man who loves his parents," he began. "A man who treats his partner gently. Who serves God, not performatively, but in his actions. A man who helps others because he wants to—not because he needs applause." A pause….then he continued, "… love is all of that. It conquers everything. It lasts. And it's more important than bank accounts and boardrooms….I added the boardrooms part." He said.

My inhale was sharp.

"Gabriel… don't do that to me."

There was a pause. Soft. Curious.

"Do what?" he asked gently.

"Don't tell me things that make you sound like the kind of man who actually listens and takes to heart the words I say," I breathed. "Because it means you're more perfect than I thought. And that is… a lot."

A quiet exhale on his end — like I'd hit him in the center of everything.

My pulse skipped.

"Maybe that's a good thing," he whispered.

A long, intimate silence followed — the kind that wasn't empty, but full. Both of us were filled with things neither of us was ready to say out loud just yet.

Then:

"Nathan?"

"Yeah?"

"I want to see you."

My whole body warmed like someone had flipped a switch behind my ribs.

"You will."

"When?" he asked, breath unsteady now — vulnerable in a way that startled me.

"When you tell me you're ready."

Another silence. Tender. Fragile. Full of promise.

Then: "…Soon," he murmured.

And the call ended — not abruptly, but like a held breath finally released.

I just lay there in my brand-new bedroom afterward, staring at the ceiling, wondering how a 20-minute phone call could make someone rethink the entire architecture of their emotional life.

I barely slept.

I floated.

I replayed every line, every laugh, every crack in his voice.

And by morning, Hailey and Marcus were at my door like two vultures sniffing for romantic gossip.

(17) When Safety is a Story You Tell Yourself

Two days. Forty-eight hours.

That was supposed to be the only inconvenience — me shuffling down the hallway wrapped in a towel, knocking on Hailey's door to use her bathroom and as much shampoo and conditioner as I could because my bathroom was barricaded behind curing sealant and I was all out of my fancy shampoo.

To my surprise?

It was… fun.

Ridiculous, inconvenient, mildly undignified — but fun. We became a chaotic little morning triage unit, bumping elbows as the two of us rotated through her cramped bathroom like a dysfunctional ballet troupe trying to brush, shave, steam, fluff, and blow-dry before racing out the door for the last week of training.

But the real chaos?

The interrogation.

Hailey and Marcus did NOT care about the Goldberg dinner.

Not one bit.

They didn't want to know about the food. Or the luxury room. Or Goldberg crushing my spine in a hug.

No.

They wanted the details of the *phone call.*

Every single second.

Nathan, what did he say? Did he flirt? How did he SOUND? Warm? Deep? Smooth? Did he ask you out or soft-launch ask you out? Did you flirt BACK? Tell me EXACTLY—word-for-word—everything!

It was like being waterboarded with friendship.

And I… Well, I was glowing.

Actually glowing.

Marcus squinted at me while brushing his teeth. "You're smiling like you swallowed a lightbulb."

Hailey bumped my hip, grinning like a sister in on a secret. "Oh, he's gone. He's *gone*. Nathan is in loooove."

I groaned into my towel.

But they weren't wrong.

Monday morning arrived, and I practically *danced* out of the apartment.

"My bathroom is READY tonight," I kept saying like it was a national holiday. "I'm gonna have the shower of my LIFE."

Hailey rolled her eyes. Marcus saluted me. But they were happy for me.

And I was happy for me too.

Final week of training. The home stretch. The world felt electric, anticipatory — like something huge was coming.

But all day?

Nothing.

No message. No envelope. No limousine. Not a shadow of Gabriel's presence.

By 4 p.m., we gathered as the managers handed out our shifts for next week.

When I looked down at mine… I blinked.

Because my schedule wasn't just surprising.

It was impossible.

Regular workdays. Weekends off.

WEEKENDS OFF!!

For newbies, that's a unicorn riding a dragon through a field of four-leaf clovers. According to management, even God Himself would have to file a formal request for that schedule.

But somehow… I was the only one.

"God must love you," Hailey said.

"Or someone pulled a string," Marcus muttered.

I didn't say it out loud, but a single name ran through my mind:

Gabriel. No last name. Just the name that lingered anyway.

At 4:22, I panicked — my keys weren't in my pocket.

"I'll meet you guys in the lobby," I told them. "I left my keys at my desk."

I jogged back up.

Quiet floor. Lights humming. Desks empty.

I turned the corner… and saw movement.

A shadow. Quick. Sharp. Flitting away from my desk toward the second door.

"HEY!" I shouted before my brain caught up. "What are you doing?!"

He didn't stop. Didn't turn. Just fled down the hall and vanished through the stairwell exit.

A chill tore through me.

I was NOT following him. Nope. No way. Not trying to get murdered today.

I called my supervisor immediately. He called security.

Within minutes Hailey and Marcus arrived, pale and breathless. Security questioned me while I checked my drawers.

Nothing missing. But my keys…

"My keys aren't where I left them," I whispered.

The guard's face changed. Concern. Confusion. Possibility.

"What did he want?" Marcus asked later. "Money? Phone? Password?"

"I don't know," I said shakily. "I don't know what he thought was in my desk…"

Thirty minutes of paperwork. Incident report. Empty reassurances.

"Go home," my supervisor said. "We'll check footage and notify you."

Never a dull moment. My life was apparently allergic to dullness.

We decided to walk — fifteen minutes of decompressing, tree-lined sidewalks, and the promise of bakery treats halfway.

"That break-in dude better not be connected to your rich mystery guy," Hailey muttered.

"Or maybe he *is* the mystery guy," Marcus added with raised eyebrows.

"No," I said firmly. "Gabriel doesn't run around stairwells in hoodies and shadows."

"Are you sure?" Hailey asked. "Rich people do weird things."

"Not THAT weird."

We laughed. A little too loud. A little too nervous.

We bought pastries. Sweet distractions. Temporary comforts.

But as we approached our building…

Something in my chest tightened.

Something felt wrong.

Hailey and Marcus entered their apartment fine.

I turned toward mine.

Stopped dead.

My door was open. Not wide. Just… slightly ajar.

A cold drop of fear slid down my spine.

"No." My voice broke. "No, no, no."

I backed away heading for the lobby and dialed the apartment manager. Then Hailey. Then Marcus again.

Twenty anxious minutes later, we all stood at my doorway with the manager.

He unlocked it properly and pushed open the door the rest of the way.

We stepped inside.

And everything — EVERYTHING — fell out of place.

My bookshelf overturned. My sofa cushions were cut open like someone was searching for diamonds. Kitchen drawers dumped. New mattress sliced apart. Clothes toppled, tossed, trampled.

But worst:

On the bathroom mirror — in red, smeared strokes —

YOU'RE NEXT

My voice cracked. "Is… is that blood?"

"Lipstick, maybe," Hailey whispered. "Paint. I don't know."

Marcus swallowed. "Nathan… man… what the hell…"

I stumbled forward. My chest caved inward.

The envelope lay on the floor. Empty.

The contents were gone.

The diary. The childhood photos. The motorcycle key. The black card.

Gone.

"NO!" My voice ripped from my throat. "My diary— those were my mom's photos— those were my—"

I sank to the floor. Shaking.

Hailey knelt beside me. "It's okay, it's okay— we'll figure this out—"

But nothing was okay.

Who came into my apartment? Who knew my schedule? Who knew exactly what mattered to me?

My heart thudded painfully.

The shadow in the office. My keys moved. Did he copy them? Like in spy movies? Had he followed me home?

Then the last thought hit me so hard it knocked the breath out of me:

Was it Goldberg? The catchphrase. The timing. The weirdness. Had I misread everything? Had I eaten dinner with someone who was about to—

"No," I whispered to myself. "No, he wouldn't— he couldn't—"

But my certainty faltered.

Everything felt wrong.

Everything felt targeted.

And the one person who might have answers — the man who sent a limo, a suit, a diary, a dream, a dinner —

wasn't there.

Not at the restaurant. Not in the office. Not here.

For the first time since moving to the city…

I felt scared.

Truly scared.

"Why is this happening?" I whispered.

Hailey squeezed my hand.

Marcus stood guard near the door.

The apartment manager made a call to security who ultimately called the police.

Sirens wailed outside.

And in that moment — in the middle of a destroyed apartment, a violated life, and a stolen dream —

One thought rose loud and clear:

I need Gabriel. Wherever he is. Whoever he is. I need him now.

(18) A Shadow in the Light

Everything froze. Time didn't just slow — it staggered, crawled, gasped.

Fear sat heavy in the room, thick as the dust being lifted off my destroyed belongings. Anger simmered under my skin like heat from a cracked volcano. Confusion wrapped around me like chains.

Police moved through the apartment in a blur of gloves, cameras, and hushed radios. I sat on the edge of my overturned couch, arms folded tightly across my chest, legs shaking uncontrollably.

They asked questions. I answered automatically. I felt like my soul stayed behind in the doorway while my body just went through motions.

The worst part? I kept glancing toward the bathroom mirror. Toward the red letters smeared across the glass.

YOU'RE NEXT

The words burned themselves into my mind.

Finally, an officer said, "Mr. Moffett, please come with us. We need you to view the surveillance feed."

My gut twisted.

I followed them to the small office downstairs, where two officers hovered over a monitor. A third stood behind me, arms folded across a bulletproof vest.

"Let's see if anything pops up," one said.

And the video rolled.

Minutes passed. Nothing. My heart quieted for a fragile moment.

Then—

At 4:00 p.m., a tall man stepped out of the front entrance.

The footage was grainy, but his height was clear. His stride. His posture. His shoes—clean, polished, expensive.

He wore:

- a long black coat
- dark clothing underneath
- a cap pulled low
- a mask covering half his face

I felt my stomach drop.

"That's him," the officer said. "We're canvassing the floor now."

Reports trickled in. Eight neighbors said nothing suspicious happened.

Typical.

It left exactly four possibilities:

Me. Marcus. Hailey. And… Roger.

Quiet, timid Roger who lived at the end of the hall and always jumped when you said hi too enthusiastically.

When the police knocked on his door, his hands were visibly shaking.

"Sir," the officer said gently, "did you see anyone near Mr. Moffett's apartment this afternoon?"

Roger swallowed. Then swallowed again.

He was terrified.

"I… yes…" he whispered. "But… I didn't want to say anything because… I didn't know if he'd come back."

The officer softened his tone. "Sir, it's very important. You did nothing wrong."

Roger wrung his hands. Tears shimmered in his eyes.

"At around 3:30," he whispered, "I saw… someone. A tall man. With a long black coat. A face mask. He had dark hair under a cap… brownish-dark eyes… he looked at me, just for a second… and I—"

He choked.

"—I panicked. I ran inside. I locked my bedroom door. I didn't come out."

The officer nodded. "You didn't follow him or look through your peephole?"

"No," Roger whispered, mortified. "I… couldn't. I—I froze."

And in that moment, oddly, painfully — I didn't blame him.

Fear does strange things to people. Fear had done strange things to me all night.

The timeline formed in my mind like a cold puzzle:

3:30 PM — the intruder enters my apartment. 4:00 PM — he leaves the building. 4:25 PM — I see a different shadow in my office, running away from my desk.

I felt a cold sweat break across my back.

"They were two different people," I whispered.

The officer nodded. "That's what it looks like."

A chill ran through me.

Whoever broke into my apartment… was NOT the person who was near my desk later.

Two men. Two intrusions. Two motives. None of which made sense.

I rubbed my temples. "This doesn't—none of this—why would someone break in *twice*?"

"Maybe the second one was startled by you," the officer said. "Came looking for something still leftover from the first intrusion."

"But nothing is missing… except…" My voice cracked.

Except my heart's secrets.

My diary. My childhood photos. The motorcycle key. The card. Gone.

Everything connected to Gabriel—gone.

The officer flipped to a new page in his notebook. "You mentioned a phrase on your mirror? Something about a wrestler?"

My throat tightened. "Goldberg. His catchphrase used to be 'Who's Next,' and in the later years… 'You're Next.' And… I had dinner with him several nights ago."

The officer raised an eyebrow. "Well, I doubt he's still here. I personally escorted him to the airport Sunday night myself. He flew to Florida for a live taping."

"Are you sure?" I forced out.

"Absolutely. He was on a televised program this afternoon. He couldn't have been here at 3:30."

I stared at the ground.

Something cold and metallic settled in my stomach.

Then I pushed past the officers and stepped back into my ruined apartment one more time, fists clenched at my sides.

"I was told not to touch anything," I said. "I won't. But I need to look."

The officer nodded.

I walked through the chaos slowly, scanning the floor, the shelves, the couch stuffing strewn like snow.

I examined the bathroom mirror again. Red paint or lipstick — the color too bright for dried blood, thank God.

Everything felt poisoned. Violated. Wrong.

I turned to leave.

And then—

Something on the tile caught my eye.

Small. Shimmering. Colorful.

Just a corner. Just an edge.

But familiar.

Very familiar.

I knelt.

A torn piece of Gabriel's restaurant card. The corner with the date and time. The tiny, elegant print.

Saturday. 7:00 PM.

My breath left my chest in a hollow ache.

The rest of the card — gone.

This one piece — left behind.

Whether by accident.

Or on purpose.

I held it between two fingers and stared at it.

"What does it mean?" I whispered.

No one answered.

But deep inside me, a truth stirred:

This wasn't random. This wasn't burglary. This wasn't chance.

Someone had taken everything connected to Gabriel.

Someone else had tried to find something at my desk.

And the only clue they left behind…

Was an invitation to the night he didn't show up.

(19) The Man in the Helmet

The officers moved around my apartment like busy shadows, radios crackling softly, pens tapping against clipboards as they documented every overturned object, every fingerprint smudge, every trace of intrusion.

I stood in the middle of it all, clutching the torn corner of a business card I'd found near the door — the card that absolutely should *not* have been there. My hands shook around it.

Fear sat heavy in my chest.

But beneath the fear — beneath the hollow numbness — There was something else beginning to rise:

I need answers.

I needed to talk to someone who could understand the gravity of this. Someone who knew more than they were allowed to say. Someone who had shown, over and over, that he knew things before I did. I needed Gabriel.

"Mr. Moffett," the lead officer said gently, "we strongly recommend you stay with a friend tonight. Or let us move you to a secure hotel until morning. You shouldn't be alone."

Hailey stepped toward me, worry in her eyes.

But my mind was already moving in a different direction.

"The restaurant," I whispered. "Gabriel's restaurant. Someone there knew he wasn't coming that night. They talked to him. They saw him. They'd know if something's wrong, or where he went after—"

"Nathan—" Hailey started, reaching for me.

I stepped back, shaking my head.

"I need answers," I repeated. "I can't just… stand here while my apartment looks like a crime scene. He knows things. He always knows things."

"Nathan!" Marcus called. "Wait—! Just wait a second—"

But I couldn't.

Didn't.

The panic, the urgency, the need to understand — it all pushed me forward harder than grief or heartbreak ever could.

I grabbed my jacket off the overturned chair and strode toward the door.

The moment the elevator opened, I was already pulling out my phone. My fingers trembled as I typed.

Nathan ➤ Gabriel: *Where are you? There's a problem at my apartment. Call me. Please.*

Then I opened the rideshare app with my other hand.

I didn't want to hear arguments. Didn't want another officer suggesting "protocols." Didn't want Hailey's worried voice, or Marcus's confusion.

I needed him. I needed someone who knew more than the police could ever tell me. Someone who had been one step ahead since I met him. I hit "Confirm Ride." The elevator dinged. The doors slid open—And I stepped into the cool air of the lobby, still typing a second message.

Nathan ➤ Gabriel: *I need to talk to you. I'm heading to the restaurant.*

I walked fast. Almost running. Through the glass doors—Out onto the sidewalk—Phone in hand, heart pounding—And right as I raised my arm to flag down my Uber, a low hum vibrated through the night.

A motorcycle engine. Slow. Controlled. Familiar.

I looked up—And froze.

A tall figure sat astride a black motorcycle at the curb. Helmet. Dark jacket. Still as a statue.

Watching me. Waiting. And even before he lifted the visor—I knew.

It was the black helmet on the tall figure wearing a tailored suit, and a long dark coat flowing behind him like the wing of some fallen angel.

His head snapped toward me — swift, precise, predatory.

And he stood with a slow and deliberate measure without taking a single step forward, without raising his voice, or gesturing wildly. Instead…He held out a helmet.

My breath vanished. Everything inside me — fear, longing, anger, confusion, desire — collided into white-hot static.

I walked to him on instinct, not sense. My hands shook as I took the helmet.

And when he reached forward, grabbed my wrist, and pulled me onto the bike — smoothly, firmly, expertly —

My body obeyed him without hesitation. I didn't wait for permission. My body obeyed without question.

The seat vibrated beneath us as the engine purred. His scent — something dark and clean and expensive — hit me like a drug.

I wrapped my arms around his waist, expecting to feel something cold or angular, a gun or a weapon or something that would confirm every fear I'd just lived through.

But instead—

I felt the hard line of his abs burning through his clothes.

I nearly passed out.

"Ohhhh—" I gasped without meaning to.

Shame flickered. Desire punched me square in the chest.

The bike lurched forward and I clutched him tighter, my fingers locking into the back of his jacket as the city blurred. Then— through the internal speakers of the helmet—soft, smooth, and impossibly intimate—

His voice slid into my ears like warm velvet.

"Finally… you're mine."

That's what I *heard*.

And just like that, my mind politely excused itself from the disaster back at the apartment. My heart slammed into a wall. My thoughts scattered. Knight in shining—no—*black* armor. Rescue. Fate. Clearly, I was moments away from a dramatic life pivot.

What he actually said was—

"Finally… you're riding with me."

He said it again.

"Hello? Are you with me in there? I said finally, you're riding with me. We have to hurry."

Reality snapped back into place like a rubber band.

Gabriel's tone dropped all urgency now. "This turn of events is dangerous. People are suspecting foul play. But it's not me, Nathan. And it's not my friend… Mr. Goldberg."

Another voice echoed inside my memory — a faint song from an old black-and-white movie playing in some corner of my childhood.

"Heaven… I'm in heaven…"

My brain melted.

My heart soared.

Then, sharply —My survival instinct slapped me across the face.

NATHAN. FOCUS. THIS. IS. LIFE. OR. DEATH.

Gabriel accelerated, tires screaming across the pavement as the city lights streaked past us.

"Hold tighter," he said.

I did. Oh God, I did. No hesitation, no restraint — fingers clutching his coat, arms locked around him.

I had never held anyone like that. Never held someone who felt like power and warmth and danger and safety all at once.

"We're going to Sogno Toscano," Gabriel said. "For answers."

My throat tightened behind the helmet.

"Gabriel— what's going on? Who broke into my apartment? Who—"

"Not now," he said gently, but firmly. "We talk when you're safe. And where we're going— You'll be safe with me."

The bike roared through the streets. Wind whipped my suit jacket. My helmet vibrated with the force of the speed.

And for the first time since the break-in…

I felt something like hope dipped in fear and stained with longing.

All tangled into something electric.

I pressed my forehead against his back, breathing in the faint scent of cedar and citrus.

For a moment — just a moment — the world felt like it was narrowing to him and me and the dark road ahead.

"Gabriel…" I whispered.

"Yes?" His voice curled into my ears like a promise.

I shuddered.

"I'm scared."

He squeezed my wrist — firm, grounding.

"Don't be," he said softly. "I've got you now."

And the city swallowed us whole.

(20) The Attempted Kiss

The motorcycle eased to a low growl as we approached Gabriel's Sogno Toscano, its engine rumbling like a predator reluctantly returning to its lair. My teeth chattered from more than just the night wind whipping through my jacket. Nerves twisted coldly in my stomach like restless sea serpents. The building loomed ahead in darkness, every window black except for a single amber light bleeding weakly from beneath the front awning.

The place didn't feel merely closed; it felt abandoned, haunted, profoundly wrong.

Gabriel guided us toward the shadowed side entrance and killed the engine. Silence rushed in thick and heavy as we coasted to a silent stop on momentum alone.

Before I could draw a full breath, something shifted at the corner of my vision—sharp and deliberate.

A man detached himself from the darkness.

He wasn't a staff member or a host. He wore a black tactical vest, carried an assault rifle slung low across his chest, and sported an earpiece that caught the faint light. He moved with the same solid authority as the stone walls around us.

My knees nearly gave way beneath me.

He closed the distance to Gabriel in three quiet strides and leaned in close enough that I barely caught the murmur. "He's here, sir. He's been waiting inside."

My pulse surged into overdrive. Someone waited in a locked-down luxury restaurant at this hour, surrounded by men armed with military-grade hardware.

Gabriel pulled off his helmet in one smooth motion. My lungs simply forgot their purpose.

He was devastating. Dark hair tumbled loose across his forehead, still wind-tousled from the ride. His eyes carried the warm, molten color of brandy caught in late-afternoon sunlight—

dangerous and inviting at once. A sharp jaw could have cut glass, and his smooth, golden-toned skin spoke of money, Mediterranean light, and effortless control. Beneath that polished surface lay something rawer, something that looked suspiciously like longing.

He turned toward me, and the entire world cracked open along a fault line.

His gloved fingers brushed my cheek as he gently lifted my helmet away. The brief skin-to-skin contact sent heat racing through me like gasoline meeting a spark. My knees dissolved into warm liquid.

I remained upright only because gravity seemed too embarrassed to let me collapse at his feet like some lovesick Regency heroine.

Those brandy eyes searched mine with deep, unblinking intensity. "Nathan," he whispered, shaping my name like a secret he had held for far too long. The sound of it made my chest ache.

"I hope I'm reading this correctly," he murmured, stepping just close enough that I felt the warmth radiating from his body. "And that you won't hate me afterward. But I need this more than ever right now."

I blinked while my brain scrambled to catch up. "Need what exactly—?"

His hand rose, warm palm cupping the side of my jaw, thumb tracing the edge of my lower lip. He leaned in slowly.

Time thickened into syrup around us.

My hands flew up on pure instinct, palms pressing flat against his chest to stop him an inch from my mouth. "Whoa—hold on there, Kemosabe." My voice cracked somewhere between laughter and panic. "You're not the Lone Ranger, and I'm absolutely not Tonto. Before anybody claims lips or anything else, I'd like you to meet my parents first—properly. Besides, beyond a kiss, I'm only interested in something platonic right now. That's where I stand."

He exhaled in a shaky, ragged breath that sounded beautifully human. The rawness of it nearly undid me completely.

"I understand," he whispered, voice low and rough around the edges. "And I respect it completely." His hand lingered one heartbeat longer before falling away, but his eyes never left mine—soft, steady, and a little wrecked.

I stood frozen while my mouth opened and closed like a fish pulled from water. I had just blocked a kiss I desperately wanted. What on earth was wrong with me?

I had told him I wanted him to meet my parents first—as if they still held veto power over my love life at almost thirty. Yet the instinct felt honorable, right somehow. I was trying—really trying—to keep something sacred, to avoid rushing into fire simply because it felt warm.

While I spiraled internally, Gabriel turned toward the back entrance with his shoulders set in quiet determination.

"I'm coming with you," I blurted, then raised my voice sharply. "Together—whatever waits inside that room, we face it together."

His lips twitched into the beginning of a smile. "Oh no, you're not," he answered in a mild, almost fond tone. "You're staying in the SUV with my detail."

I barked a laugh that sounded borderline manic. "Um, absolutely not."

One dark brow arched in silent question.

"I'm ready," I declared, stepping closer while adrenaline lifted my voice. "Ready to kick someone's ass if they even look at you wrong. I don't care if I forget their name later—don't start a fight if you can't handle Nathan's wrath. They came for you? Fine. But they messed with me too when they ruined this night. So it's on like Donkey Kong, baby."

Gabriel actually choked on a half-laugh, half-cough.

"Your nostalgic 80s references are going to be the death of me," he muttered, eyes dancing despite the tension surrounding us.

He gave the rifle-bearing guard a subtle nod. The man stepped forward without a word, unclipped a compact metal case from his vest, and flipped it open. Inside lay a sleek black handgun—compact, deadly, and unmistakably professional.

He offered it with both hands in a formal gesture.

I accepted it. My fingers trembled, not from fear now, but from pure electric adrenaline.

"Thanks," I breathed.

Gabriel settled his hand warm and steady at the small of my back. "You stay right with me," he instructed in a low, final tone. "No matter what happens. Understood?"

"Understood."

We moved forward slowly and deliberately. Cold night air slid over my skin like silk gloves.

Inside, *Gabriel's Sogno Toscano* resembled a mausoleum of Italian opulence—marble floors gleamed dully, velvet drapes hung heavy, and unlit candles waited like patient ghosts.

We reached the private dining corridor. Gabriel lifted one finger to his lips in a clear signal for silence.

He reached for the heavy curtain—the same one I had waited behind alone days earlier, heart lodged in my throat. He drew it back inch by slow inch.

Warm golden light spilled outward, flickering and intimate. Candle flames danced across crystal and linen.

Seated alone in the center, bathed in that single pool of light, was Bill Goldberg.

He appeared massive, armored in black tactical fabric stretched tight over granite muscle. His jaw locked tightly, his brow furrowed deeply enough to hide secrets, and his expression carried the sharpness of a blade.

He smirked—not in friendliness or cruelty, but with slow, knowing certainty that said he had been waiting and remained entirely unimpressed.

He leaned back in the high-backed chair, thick arms folding across his chest with deliberate menace.

"Well," he rumbled in a voice like gravel dragged over concrete, "it's about damn time you two showed up."

(21) Old Enemies, New Targets

The candlelight made the shadows dance across Goldberg's shoulders, making him look even bigger than he already was. He sat forward in his chair like a linebacker ready to charge, while Gabriel hovered beside me—calm, sharp, coiled like someone preparing for impact.

Goldberg broke the silence first.

"So," he said, voice gravel-deep, "I hear you've had an interesting week."

I let out a breath that sounded halfway between a laugh and a sigh.

"Interesting? Let's see…" I counted on my fingers. "Dinner with you. A surprise luxury apartment makeover. A break-in. My desk was tampered with. And a psychopath with a Sharpie complex writing messages on my mirror." I spread my hands. "So yeah, Bill, 'interesting' works."

He grunted — not unsympathetic.

"But what I really want to know," I pressed, looking between them, "is why you're here. Why are we meeting in the dark at Gabriel's restaurant? Why is there a guy with a rifle outside?"

Goldberg glanced at Gabriel.

Gabriel exhaled, long and slow. "Because," he said, "an old enemy of mine has resurfaced."

I blinked. "Who?"

Gabriel's expression hardened — controlled, but shadowed in a way I'd never seen before.

"His name," he said quietly, "is Calvin Marshall."

The name hit the air like a crack of thunder — sharp, unfamiliar, full of weight I couldn't yet understand.

Gabriel took a seat across from me. Goldberg leaned back, arms crossed.

And I listened.

"Years ago," Gabriel began, "when I was just starting out, Calvin was one of the most successful businessmen in the state. He owned multiple companies, inherited old money, and had a hand in everything from finance to shipping."

Goldberg nodded. "He had power. Too much power. And he liked to remind people of it."

"He saw potential in me," Gabriel continued. "Back when I had very little. He financed one of my early ventures, helped me get the capital I needed." He paused. "In the beginning, he wasn't the villain. Or maybe I just didn't see it."

"What happened?" I asked.

Gabriel's eyes flickered with something that hurt to look at.

"When the financial crisis hit in '89, he changed. He became controlling… obsessive. Every decision I made, every deal, every new direction — he wanted control over all of it. He tried to dictate my business as if I were his puppet."

"And Gabe told him to shove it," Goldberg said proudly.

Gabriel didn't even crack a smile.

"We parted ways," he said. "Violently. I rebuilt my empire from scratch, paid him back far more than I owed, and walked away. My independence infuriated him."

"That's putting it lightly," Goldberg snorted. "He lost money. A lot of it. And he blamed Gabriel. Not the economy. Not his decisions. Just Gabe."

Gabriel's gaze went distant.

"He swore he'd come for me someday. And he did. First quietly… then openly. He attacked my business. My reputation." A pause. "My family."

My breath hitched.

"And me," Goldberg added. "He tried to knock out my early football prospects, sabotage deals, wreck my wrestling debut before it even got started."

I stared between them — horror, confusion, and clarity dawning all at once.

"And now," I said slowly, "he's back."

Gabriel nodded once.

"And he's using *you* as leverage," he said. "To draw me out. To shake me. To create chaos."

My heartbeat thudded in my throat.

"But… the break-in," I whispered, "who did that?"

This time Gabriel didn't answer.

He reached into a small leather pouch on the table and slid it toward me.

I opened it.

My breath left my lungs.

Inside were:

- My diary
- My childhood photos
- The motorcycle key
- The black restaurant card

Everything I thought was stolen. Everything I thought the intruder took.

I stared up at Gabriel.

"You… were in my apartment?" I asked softly. "You were the first one?"

"Yes," he admitted. "At 3:30 p.m. I got in, took the items for your safety, and got out. I didn't touch anything else. I didn't destroy anything."

"So, the person who came later…" I swallowed hard. "That wasn't you. That was Calvin."

"Exactly," Gabriel said. "He found your house key — the one he duplicated at your desk earlier — and used it to get into your apartment."

Goldberg added, "And he tried to frame me by using my old catchphrase. Bastard's got a taste for theatrics."

I shivered, remembering the red message on the mirror.

"You're Next."

"And now," Gabriel said quietly, "we know he's escalating."

"But why now?" I asked. "Why me? Why target you through me?"

Gabriel and Goldberg exchanged a look — one I couldn't decipher.

Finally Gabriel spoke.

"Because you're someone he can get to. You're new. You're unsuspecting. You're close to me."

My chest tightened.

"And… because he wants to hurt me," Gabriel finished. "And you matter to me."

I froze.

Gabriel didn't look away and definitely didn't try to retract or soften it.

Goldberg cleared his throat.

"And there's one more thing," he said, leaning forward. "Calvin isn't acting alone. Not this time."

Gabriel tensed.

"What do you mean?" he asked.

"I mean," Goldberg said slowly, "someone close to you —
someone in your world, your circle — is feeding him information.
Setting you up. And framing me at the same time."

My mouth went dry.

Gabriel's voice turned dangerous.

"And you're certain?"

Goldberg nodded. "I'm damn certain. And I've got evidence."

The room fell heavy around us — thick, weighted with betrayal
I didn't yet understand.

My voice came out small, exhausted.

"Who?" I asked. "Bill… who?"

Goldberg took a breath—

(22) The Mole in the Walls

Silence hung thick over the table, broken only by the low hum of the lights overhead.

Bill leaned back, crossed his arms, and stared at Gabriel with that look of someone about to drop a bomb.

"Remember when you asked me to have dinner with Nathan because you were tending to… *urgent matters*?" Bill asked.

"I remember," Gabriel said slowly. "Why?"

"Well…" Bill scratched his jaw. "When I came in the back way—your hidden entrance—you know, the one by the cold storage? Yeah. I overheard something."

Gabriel's eyes narrowed.

"That's when I heard your head waiter, Lopez," Bill continued, "having a nice little phone conversation with your old friend Calvin. And by 'nice,' I mean slimy. He told Calvin your new squeeze—Nathan—was arriving soon, and that I'd be there to keep him company. Mentioned you were hot on Calvin's trail. Real helpful guy."

My stomach turned.

Gabriel's jaw flexed. Hard.

Bill wasn't done.

"So it looks like Mr. Lopez is a mole with expensive taste and terrible instincts. And since you weren't here, Gabe, I took matters into my own hands."

Gabriel blinked. "What did you do?"

Bill whistled with a loud and sharp penetrating sound. The curtain parted instantly.

Two security guards marched in, dragging a shivering Juan Lopez between them. He was handcuffed, gagged, and pale — limbs stiff, skin tinged with cold.

"Kept him on ice for a couple of hours," Bill said casually, nodding toward the back. "In the fridge. Doesn't kill 'em, apparently. Just turns 'em into truth-flavored popsicles."

Gabriel's eyes darkened with a rage I'd never seen from him.

"Ah… Mr. Juan Lopez," Gabriel said, voice like calm before a hurricane. "This is how you repay me? I took you out of Venezuela. I gave you a job. Raises. Benefits. A villa. And this is the loyalty I get?"

He flicked two fingers, and the guard removed the gag.

Lopez gasped, jaw trembling violently.

"You don't understaaaand—" he stammered, accent thick with fear. "Calvin… he came… he came here one day. Asking questions. Shoving money into pockets. He had a gun. He said he'd kill us if we didn't help."

"He would've killed you anyway," Gabriel snapped.

Lopez shook harder. "He told me to find out where you were. Who were you seeing. When I mentioned Nathan, he kept me alive. Said he wanted to know everything about him. Everything about your relationship." His teeth chattered. "He gave me money. Promised not to shoot me. Told me to call him as soon as Nathan and Goldberg arrived."

Gabriel closed his eyes. Exhaled once. Then with a slowed voice yet deadly poised way about him,

"Lopez… you should've taken the bullet."

He looked up sharply at the man he once trusted.

"You betrayed me. Worse — you endangered the people I care about."

Something inside me snapped.

I stepped forward. Not shaking. Not scared.

Just furious.

"You put ME on his radar," I said, voice low. "You gave up Gabriel. You gave up Bill. You gave up our lives for a few thousand bucks and a threat you didn't have the spine to stand up to."

Lopez tried to shrink in on himself.

I didn't let him.

"You could've gotten all of us killed. All of us. And then what, pendejo? No job. No villa. No life. Nothing."

My hand lifted the gun before I even registered the movement.

BAM. BAM. Two shots. Clean. Precise. Straight through both knees. Lopez screamed and collapsed, legs folding inward. Bill's eyes went wide.

"Damn, kid," he barked. "That's badass."

Gabriel stared at me like he was seeing a new dimension of who I was.

"I chose Nathan correctly," he said quietly. "Judge Dredd, apparently." His smirk ghosted in the candlelight. "He knows how to make consequences count. But… Nathan…"

He nodded toward Lopez on the floor.

"It wasn't just two lives he endangered."

Something in me sharpened. Clicked.

"Oh, right," I murmured. "There *were* three."

I raised the gun one more time.

BAM.

Lopez's scream shot up into the ceiling as he curled into himself, clutching what was left of the third target between his legs.

Bill winced sympathetically. Gabriel just nodded, satisfied.

"There," I said, lowering the gun. "That's three."

His mouth twitched—not a smile. Something darker.

"He understands consequences."

Then his gaze dropped to Lopez.

"But consequences don't require a body count."

Something in me loosened. Just a fraction.

Gabriel turned to the guards.

"Take him out the back. Call the vet. We need some grooming done."

Lopez wailed as they dragged him away, blood streaking the marble, dignity already gone.

When the curtain fell behind him, the silence was immediate. Dense. Changed.

Bill finally broke it.

"Alright," he said, straightening his jacket. "We're cleaning this up. Camera loop, shell casings gone, and we make damn sure Nathan isn't anywhere near the official version of tonight."

I swallowed.

Gabriel turned to him.

"He never fired the weapon and the GSR residue will be as good as gone," Gabriel said evenly. "He reacted. I handled the rest."

His eyes flicked back to me—protective now. Unyielding.

"Understood?"

Bill nodded once.

"Understood."

Top of Form

Bottom of Form

Bill pulled out a thin folder. Tossed it on the table.

"Because Calvin's not done," he said. "He's not alone. And the next person he's going after…"

He tapped the folder.

"…is sitting at this table."

(23) The Bait Worth Killing For

The folder Bill threw on the table sat there like a ticking bomb. I stared at it, throat tight, pulse in my teeth.

Bill didn't touch it again. He didn't have to.

"Open it," Gabriel said quietly.

My fingers trembled as I cracked the folder open.

Inside were:

- Surveillance stills
- Printouts of intercepted messages
- A list of financial transfers
- And a final sheet with my full name printed in red ink.

I felt my stomach plummet.

Gabriel reached out, steadying my wrist as I held the papers.

"He's not coming after all three of us," Bill said. "He's coming after *you.*"

I swallowed hard.

"Why?" I whispered. "Why me? I'm… nobody special."

Both men stared at me as if I'd just said something blasphemous.

Gabriel leaned forward, voice low, urgent, *certain.*

"No, Nathan. You're everything he's been denied. Everything he can't have."

My heart hiccupped.

Bill nodded, expression grim.

"See, Calvin's been without real loyalty for decades," he said. "No family left who trusts him. No partner. No friend. No one who shows up for him unless they're paid to."

"He doesn't understand love," Gabriel added. "He doesn't understand loyalty unless it's bought. And he hates, hates, *hates* that I found someone who gives those things freely."

My breath caught.

Gabriel's gaze deepened. "He sees you as a threat. A symbol. The new beginning I chose — without him."

Bill pointed at the surveillance still — a grainy shot of Calvin pacing outside Gabriel's condo tower days ago.

"To him, you're the new investment Gabriel made," Bill said. "A living reminder that Gabe rebuilt better without him. Laughing again. Living again. Hell — even loving again."

I flushed, throat tightening. Gabriel didn't deny it.

"He wants you," Bill continued, "because if he gets you, he gets Gabe on his knees."

Silence punched the air between us.

I felt sick. Cold. Shaking.

"So… what do we do?" I whispered.

Gabriel sat back, hands steepled, eyes sharp and calculating — the mind of a man who ran empires…and now had something to lose.

"We put you somewhere," he said slowly, "that Calvin can't resist."

Bill cracked his knuckles.

"Somewhere he'll rush into without thinking."

"Somewhere," Gabriel added, "that forces him to take the bait."

My pulse hammered. "You want to use me," I said quietly, "as bait."

"No," Gabriel said firmly, leaning across the table. "I don't want to. But it's the only way to draw him out before he hurts you."

My voice trembled despite myself.

"And what if he kills me before you get to him?"

Gabriel's face changed completely.

All the billionaire composure. All the stoic calm. All the distance.

Gone.

He leaned in, hands cupping my jaw, voice steady and fierce.

"I won't let that happen."

Bill nodded in agreement.

"You've got two of the most stubborn, dangerous men on the planet watching your back. Calvin comes within ten feet of you, and his ass is grass."

I sat still, heart pounding in my throat.

"Where would we even put me?" I asked.

Gabriel's eyes flickered with a spark of strategy.

"Somewhere symbolic," he said. "Somewhere Calvin knows you'd be vulnerable." "Somewhere public enough to force him to move fast… but controlled enough that we're ready for him."

Bill smirked.

"And lucky for you, I know just the place."

Gabriel turned to him sharply.

"Where?"

Bill's smirk widened into something sly.

"Nathan's apartment." He paused. "Or what *used* to be his apartment."

Bill wanted to put me back at my apartment.

"It's familiar. Secure. Easier to control," he said, already reaching for his phone.

I shook my head.

"Not there," I said.

He looked up.

"Then where?"

"My parents' place," I said. "The farmhouse."

Bill paused.

"You've got neighbors."

"Three," I said. "All about a mile out. Different road."

Gabriel glanced at me.

"Visibility?"

"None," I answered. "Trees, heavy foliage. You don't see the house unless you already know it's there."

Bill considered that.

"So no casual traffic."

"Exactly," I said. "And no reason for anyone to come looking."

Bill exhaled slowly.

"You're assuming Calvin won't move fast."

Gabriel spoke without hesitation.

"He won't," he said.

Bill turned to him.

"You sure?"

Gabriel nodded once.

"Calvin plans," he said. "He tests. If we disappear quietly for a few days, he'll hesitate. He'll wait to see what we do next."

His eyes flicked briefly to me.

"And while we're quiet," Gabriel added, "we may be able to pick up his trail when he moves."

The farmhouse wasn't just a hiding place.

It was layered.

Off the main road. Shielded by trees. Close enough to civilization to be normal—far enough to disappear.

"It'll be peaceful," I said. "And we can leave fast if we need to."

Bill studied us both.

"I still think Calvin acts sooner than you want him to."

Gabriel's voice didn't change.

"Then we'll already be gone."

A long beat.

Bill nodded.

"Alright. Farmhouse."

Gabriel was already making calls.

Private vehicles. No fixed pattern. A lean security detail that wouldn't draw attention.

Hailey and Marcus were prepped and moved quietly.

Someone was assigned to watch my apartment building while we were gone—eyes on the doors, nothing flashy.

As we stepped outside, Gabriel leaned close.

"I like this," he said.

I smiled.

"Wait until you see it."

(24) The Moffett Farm

The trip wasn't far—maybe an hour under normal circumstances—but that estimate didn't account for Hailey's bladder, which appeared to be roughly the size of a pea, or Marcus's chocolate cravings, which seemed to intensify the farther we drove from civilization.

Pit stops happened. Frequently.

Hailey apologized every time. Marcus never did.

Gabriel bore it with impressive restraint, though I caught his jaw flex more than once as another gas station sign loomed into view. The security detail, to their credit, blended seamlessly—plain clothes, ordinary vehicles, no telltale posture or presence that screamed *armed and alert*. If I hadn't known better, I would've thought we were just another small group on a road trip.

Still, Gabriel hated the stops.

Too many cameras. Too many accidental records.

By the third delay, he finally spoke up. "Everyone," he said evenly, "please hold your urine and your cravings. We need to get there."

No one argued.

When we finally turned onto the familiar road and the farmhouse appeared—half-hidden by trees and foliage, just the way it always had—I felt something in my chest ease. The vehicles repositioned automatically, angled for a quick exit if needed, and a quiet perimeter sweep was ordered before anyone stepped out.

"Well look at *this*," my mother said, hands on her hips. "You disappear for months and come back with… a whole entourage."

Sadie took that as her cue and launched herself forward.

"Sadie—no—Sadie—!" my dad called, far too late.

She bolted straight for Gabriel, tail whipping like a propeller, nose pressed firmly to his leg.

"Well," Gabriel said mildly, glancing down as she licked his hand, "I appear to have passed inspection."

Mom squinted at him. "Oh, she doesn't do that for just anyone."

"That's good to hear," Gabriel replied. "I'd hate to think I wasn't special."

Dad laughed. "I like him already."

I sighed. "Traitors. Both of you."

Sadie exploded into the yard like she'd been fired from a cannon.

She bolted past the guards, tail wagging violently, nose working overtime, dispensing friendly licks and enthusiastic nudges as if she'd personally invited herself onto the security team. The tension cracked instantly.

Mom and Dad followed, smiling so wide it hurt to look at them.

Their eyes kept lingering on Gabriel—longer than polite— clearly cataloging his height, his composure, his *very unfairly handsome face*. I hadn't told them about him yet. I could tell they were already suspicious.

They adored Hailey and Marcus immediately. Everyone gravitated toward the porch like it was magnetic. Chairs scraped. Lemonade appeared. Someone handed Marcus a cookie he absolutely had not earned yet. Within minutes, stories were being exchanged, laughter bouncing around in scattershot fashion, old familiarity wrapping around new people like it had always been meant to.

"So," Mom said, settling in, eyes bouncing between Gabriel, Hailey, and Marcus. "Let's start simple. Who are you people, and how did you all end up with *him*?"

She thumbed at me.

Hailey raised her hand. "I like him. But he's terrible under pressure."

"That's a lie," I protested.

"You panic-clean," Marcus added. "Aggressively."

Gabriel smiled and lied through his teeth so convincingly. "He alphabetized spices at my place once."

Dad nodded seriously. "That tracks."

Mom leaned forward. "And you?" she asked Gabriel. "What's your story?"

Gabriel considered her for a moment. "I met your son at a time when neither of us was looking for… company," he said carefully. "But he has a way of showing up anyway."

Mom's smile softened. "Well, you're welcome here. Anyone who keeps him out of trouble is already doing the Lord's work."

I choked on my drink.

Dad wasn't done. "Or at least makes sure he eats."

Inside, the house filled with noise. Glorious. Slightly unhinged.

Stories about me growing up—some exaggerated, some humiliatingly accurate. Old photos appeared. Awkward ones. The kind you pray never surfaces in adulthood. Questions followed: how we'd all met, how we'd ended up here together, who belonged to whom and in what way.

Dinner preparations divided us naturally. Hailey and I helped Mom in the kitchen. Marcus and Gabriel set the table with Dad. The security team was fed as well—no ceremony, no separation. Just people eating.

We sat together at the family table, sharing real food, real conversation, the kind of quiet normalcy that felt almost foreign after everything else.

"Tell them about the time you fell into the pond," Mom said.

"That was *one* time," I shot back.

Dad grinned. "You screamed."

"I slipped."

"You screamed like a haunted kettle." Dad laughed out loud.

Gabriel laughed outright, covering his mouth with his napkin.

Mom turned to him. "Oh, you should see the pictures."

"No," I said firmly. "He should not."

Too late. Dad was already up, returning with an album.

"That's him," Dad said proudly, pointing. "Right there. Bowl cut. Denim shorts."

Gabriel leaned closer, eyes sparkling. "I feel honored to witness this."

"You shouldn't," I muttered.

Mom served food like she was feeding an army. "Eat. All of you. No one leaves my table hungry."

Marcus whispered to Hailey, "I think this is how people get adopted."

Later, between bites, Mom asked casually, "So… how exactly did you all meet?"

The table quieted just a fraction.

I started. Gabriel finished. Hailey filled in the embarrassing gaps. Marcus added commentary no one requested.

By the end, Dad leaned back and nodded. "Well," he said, "that's one way to make friends."

Later, as plates were cleared and Bill called in to say the day had passed without incident—

"Tell him he's welcome anytime," Mom said loudly. "But not empty-handed."

—I realized something.

The farmhouse hadn't just hidden us.

It had *absorbed* us.

When night fell, we stayed within earshot of each other. Whispered conversations drifted through the halls.

At one point, Gabriel murmured something to me in the dark.

From another room, Hailey's sleepy voice floated back, "That's not true."

Gabriel blinked. "…Was that directed at me?"

"Yes," she said, already half asleep.

---

(25) Getting to Know

Morning came with bacon sizzling, shrill laughter, and the smell of home.

Gabriel and I wobbled down the hallway to a kitchen already alive—hashbrowns crisping, eggs cracking, pancakes flipping, sausage links browning, fruit laid out in bright, impossible colors. Laughter drifted through the house as everyone gathered around the table.

Everyone except Sadie.

"Where is she?" Mom asked, glancing toward the door. "It isn't like her. After her morning pee, she always comes straight back—especially when sausage is involved."

She paused, then shrugged. "Probably chasing a squirrel."

Breakfast continued.

By the time plates were cleared, Hailey and Marcus had volunteered for dishes, arguing cheerfully over who'd done more work. I took the opening and guided Mom and Dad toward the living room—bringing Gabriel with me. Juice and water were poured. Chairs arranged without anyone needing to say so.

My nerves kicked in immediately.

I felt like a long-tailed cat in a room full of rocking chairs.

I shared a little—about work, about how I'd met Gabriel— keeping the edges soft. Mom refilled glasses without asking. That was always her tell.

"So, Gabriel," she said casually, settling back into her chair. "You've heard all the embarrassing stories about Nathan now. Fair's fair."

Gabriel smiled politely. "I suspected this moment was coming."

Dad chuckled. "Don't worry. We don't bite. Much."

Gabriel glanced at me first—not asking permission, just checking alignment. I nodded.

"Well," Mom said gently, "where are you from?"

Gabriel exhaled through his nose, thoughtful. "A few places," he said. "Mostly places people don't stay long."

Dad lifted a brow. "Military?"

"Adjacent," Gabriel replied. "Work that moves you once you start to settle."

Right on cue, Hailey and Marcus mad-dashed in from the kitchen and dropped into seats like this was the main event.

Hailey leaned forward, elbows on her knees. "So you never had a *home* home?"

Gabriel paused. Not long—but long enough.

"I had houses," he said. "Structures. Security. Schedules." Then, quieter: "Home was… inconsistent."

Mom's expression softened immediately.

"That's a hard way to grow up," she said.

Gabriel nodded once. "It teaches you how to listen. How to read a room. How to leave before you're asked."

Dad studied him for a moment. "And what made you stop doing that?"

The room went still—not tense, just attentive.

Gabriel didn't answer right away.

I felt it before he spoke—the shift. The weight moving.

"Your son," he said simply.

Hailey made a small, satisfied sound. "Called it."

I shot her a look.

Gabriel continued, calm but unguarded. "Nathan doesn't leave rooms," he said. "He roots himself. Even when it costs him."

Mom smiled, pride unmistakable. "He always has."

Coffee was poured then—fresh, instant brewed. Chairs pulled closer. The house settled into that quiet hum it only ever had after a full breakfast—content, unhurried, safe.

Mom cradled her mug and looked at Gabriel over the rim.

"So," she said gently, "we know what Nathan was like growing up." She glanced at me, then back to him. "But we don't know anything about *you*."

Gabriel shifted slightly—not away. Just aware.

Dad leaned back on the couch. "Did you grow up around here?"

Gabriel smiled faintly. "No, sir."

"City?" Mom asked.

"Sometimes," he said. "Mostly wherever my father's work sent us."

Hailey frowned. "Was it hard? Moving all the time?"

Gabriel considered it. "It wasn't hard when you don't expect anything different," he said. "It only becomes difficult when you realize other people stayed."

Mom nodded, absorbing that.

"And your parents?" she asked. "Are they still living?"

Gabriel hesitated just a beat. "My mother passed some years ago," he said. "My father is… alive."

Dad tilted his head. "You say that like it's complicated."

Gabriel breathed out softly. "It is."

The room shifted—not heavy. Focused.

Mom didn't push. She never did.

"What were they like?" she asked instead.

Gabriel looked down at his hands, then back up.

"My father believed discipline was love," he said. "Preparation was protection. Weakness was… expensive." A pause. "My mother believed in quiet. In endurance."

Mom's eyes softened. "That's a lonely combination."

Gabriel nodded once.

Dad asked carefully, "Did you feel safe?"

The question landed deeper than any of the others.

Gabriel didn't answer right away.

And that was when the story changed hands.

Gabriel — POV

I hadn't expected to talk about them.

Not here. Not in this house that smelled like coffee and wood and something warm baking even when nothing was in the oven. Not with people who asked questions without traps hidden inside them.

Safety had never been a given in my childhood. It had been something you manufactured—through obedience, silence, anticipation.

My father taught me how to stand. How to listen. How to never need anything from anyone. My mother taught me how to disappear. I learned early that love was not loud. It was conditional. It was earned in increments and revoked without warning.

Nathan's mother had just asked me if I'd felt safe.

I realized, sitting there in her living room, that no one had ever asked me that before. Not as a child. Not as a man.

"I don't think safety was the goal," I said finally. "Capability was."

Nathan shifted beside me. I felt it without looking.

"My father wanted me prepared for the worst version of the world," I continued. "And my mother… wanted me to survive it."

I stopped there. Not because there wasn't more—but because this was enough. For now.

(26) The Ask

Dad watched Gabriel for a long moment, hands folded loosely in front of him.

"Seems like you've had it difficult, Gabriel," he said at last.

Gabriel nodded once. "It wasn't easy," he said. "But along the way, I did make choices. Some good. Some… less so." He paused, collecting himself. "I suppose now I'm trying to make the best of all of it."

Dad studied him, not unkindly.

"That usually tells you more about a man than how he started," he said.

Gabriel swallowed.

"There's something I'd like to say to you," he continued, voice steady but thinner now. "In that regard, Mr. Moffett."

I felt it immediately—the shift in him. The tension was gathering under his skin. This was the man who faced threats without blinking, who calculated risk like breathing.

And now his hand shook. Just slightly.

Gabriel cleared his throat. "I care very deeply for your son," he said. "Nathan brings… grounding to my life. Perspective. He makes rooms feel permanent." A breath. "I wanted to ask—respectfully—if you would be comfortable with me dating him."

The word landed awkwardly. Earnestly. Like he wasn't sure it belonged to him.

Silence filled the room.

Dad didn't move at first. Didn't speak.

Then he stood.

Slowly.

He crossed to the mantle and lifted the shotgun resting there, along with a small box of shells. He squinted as he opened the barrel, deliberate and unhurried, and began loading it—one shell at a time.

Click. Click.

When he finished, he snapped the barrel closed with a practiced motion. The latch clicked into place.

Gabriel's jaw tightened. He searched for words, then lost them.

"I understand if—if you have concerns," he said carefully. "I know I'm not what you expected. And I—"

"Gabriel."

Dad's voice stopped him cold.

He turned back, the shotgun resting easily against his shoulder, and studied him for a long moment.

Then Dad set the gun back on the mantle.

He stepped forward and held out his hand.

"Son," he said simply, "you're asking the right way."

Gabriel froze, then carefully took his hand.

Dad squeezed once—firm, grounding.

"You've clearly worked hard to keep your life together," Dad continued. "And anyone who looks at Nathan the way you do… well." He glanced at me. "That tells me enough."

Mom smiled quietly, wiping at the corner of her eye as she'd just caught dust.

Dad looked back at Gabriel. "If you treat him with honesty, respect, and kindness," he said, "you're welcome here."

Gabriel nodded, throat tight. "I will," he said. "I promise."

Hailey exhaled loudly. "Well. That went better than expected."

Marcus grinned. "I give it a solid ten out of ten."

I hadn't realized I was holding my breath until it left me all at once.

Gabriel sat back down slowly, hands still trembling just enough to notice.

And that was when I understood something important.

The bravest thing Gabriel had done all morning wasn't surviving his past. It was choosing to step into a future he couldn't control.

Dad clapped a hand on Gabriel's shoulder—firm, approving—then excused himself. He retrieved the shotgun and headed toward the door without ceremony, the way a man does when instinct, not fear, tells him something is off.

Something hadn't felt right all morning.

Dad felt it first. Then it spread—quietly, invisibly—through the house, like a change in pressure before a storm.

No one said anything. But everyone felt it.

Gabriel — POV

I noticed it the moment Nathan's father clapped my shoulder.

The gesture was warm. Familiar. But his hand lingered just a fraction longer than necessary—not in hesitation, but in confirmation. A man reassuring himself before acting.

Then he turned, lifted the shotgun, and walked toward the door without explanation.

No rush. No announcement.

That was what told me everything.

People who panic make noise. People who *know* move quietly.

The room didn't freeze—but it stilled. Conversations softened. Bodies adjusted without anyone quite realizing they were doing it.

Nathan felt it too. I saw it in the way his posture shifted, subtle and unconscious, the way someone who grew up here recognized a change in weather before the clouds showed themselves.

I didn't look at him.

I followed his father with my eyes instead.

I'd spent most of my life learning how to read men in motion. The set of shoulders. The economy of steps. The absence of doubt. Nathan's father wasn't afraid.

He was certain.

My hand drifted to my side as I stood, fingers brushing the concealed holster beneath my jacket. The motion was instinctive—quiet, practiced, invisible to anyone not looking for it.

The weight of the handgun grounded me.

I didn't draw it. Not yet.

I followed him to the doorway, keeping a few steps back, letting him set the pace. He glanced at me once—not surprised, not alarmed.

Just a nod.

Outside, the air felt different. Heavier. Like the land itself was holding its breath.

"Dog should've been back by now," he said calmly, eyes scanning the tree line.

I followed his gaze.

Sadie wasn't just a pet. She was an early-warning system with fur and loyalty. Animals didn't disappear without reason.

"I noticed," I said.

Nathan's father shifted the shotgun into a more comfortable hold—not threatening, just ready.

"Something's been off since dawn," he said. "Could be nothing. But I don't ignore feelings like that anymore."

Neither did I.

I stepped closer, my voice low. "If it's nothing, we lose a few minutes," I said. "If it's something, we're already too late to pretend otherwise."

That earned me a glance. Another nod.

I slipped the handgun free from its holster—not raised, not visible from the house—just present in my hand, an extension of preparation rather than intent.

Behind us, the house remained warm. Safe. Unaware.

Ahead of us, the trees stood still.

Nathan's father took the first step forward.

I followed.

Nathan's father didn't hurry.

That told me more than any alarm ever could.

We moved along the edge of the yard where the grass thinned into leaf litter and roots. He carried the shotgun low, barrel angled down, not sweeping—just present. I stayed a half step behind and to his left, handgun loose in my grip, finger indexed along the frame.

No radio chatter. No signals.

We didn't need them.

The morning sounds were wrong.

Birdsong existed, but it was sparse—too spaced out. Insects hummed, but not in chorus. The kind of quiet that didn't mean peace, just *pause*.

I scanned the tree line first. No broken branches. No crushed undergrowth. Whatever had passed through hadn't been careless.

Nathan's father stopped near the old fence post—the one leaning just enough to always look temporary. He crouched, touching the soil with two fingers.

"Tracks," he said quietly.

I joined him, careful where I placed my feet.

Dog prints. Fresh. Running hard.

Then—something else.

The stride length changed. Too long. Too even.

Human.

"Someone followed her," I said.

"Or spooked her," he replied.

We followed the line toward the woods, stopping just before the foliage thickened. The trees swallowed sound here. Light filtered in broken fragments.

I noticed it then.

The gate.

It was still closed, but the latch had been reset incorrectly. Not broken. Not forced. Just… handled by someone unfamiliar with it.

Intentional. Careful. Temporary.

Nathan's father straightened slowly.

"They didn't come for us," he said.

"No," I agreed. "They came to see if we were here."

Or to see who was.

A low sound drifted from deeper in the trees—not a bark. Not a growl.

A whine.

My chest tightened.

We moved in sync without discussion, advancing just far enough to see her.

Sadie was crouched behind a fallen log, tail tucked, one front paw lifted awkwardly. Not injured badly—but frightened. Alert. Watching something that was no longer there.

I lowered myself slowly and clicked my tongue once.

She recognized the sound instantly and scrambled toward us, pressing into Nathan's father's legs like she'd been holding her breath too long.

"She didn't chase," he murmured. "She hid."

I scanned again. The woods offered nothing obvious now—no movement, no shape out of place.

Which meant whoever had been here was already gone.

Or watching from farther out.

I holstered the handgun and pulled my phone instead, sending a single text to Bill.

Perimeter breach. No contact. The dog spooked. Signs of recon.

Nathan's father looked back toward the house.

"They didn't cross the line," he said.

"No," I replied. "They were measuring it."

He nodded grimly.

"We need to move people inside," he said. "Quietly."

"And change patterns," I added. "Now."

We turned back toward the farmhouse together, Sadie glued to his side, the morning sun suddenly too bright for how thin the margin had become.

Whatever had been watching us had learned something.

So had we.

---

(27) Watchful Encounters

Gabriel's POV

We didn't announce it.

That would've been a mistake.

Nathan's father opened the door and stepped inside as if nothing had happened, Sadie at his heel, tail low but wagging just enough to look normal. I followed a beat later, easing the door shut behind us and sliding the deadbolt into place with a soft, final click.

Inside, the house smelled like coffee and bacon and safety.

Which made the contrast sharper.

"Everything okay?" Nathan's mother asked, glancing up from the sink.

"Just checking the fence line," his father replied easily. "Dog spooked herself."

She smiled, unconcerned, and turned back to her dish towel.

Good. Keep it that way.

I caught Nathan's eye across the room and gave him a look that meant *not here*. He read it instantly and nodded once, already shifting closer to Hailey and Marcus without drawing attention.

I moved through the house the way I always did—slow, observant, unremarkable.

Windows first.

I didn't close the curtains all at once. That would've been noticed. I adjusted the blinds as if correcting glare. Rotated slats a fraction. Enough to limit angles without killing light.

Doors next.

The side entrance was locked already. I tested it anyway—solid. The mudroom door got a second deadbolt turned quietly. The back porch latch slid home with a controlled motion.

Nathan's father followed my movements without commentary. When I paused in the hallway, he drifted toward the far end of the house, posture relaxed, eyes working.

We were communicating without words.

I sent two messages while pretending to check my phone.

Perimeter recon confirmed. No contact. Locking down softly. Keep eyes on the tree line. No approach unless they cross.

Bill replied almost instantly.

Copy. Adjusting coverage. Drone high and wide.

Good.

In the living room, Hailey had curled onto the arm of the couch, Marcus beside her, both laughing at something on his phone. I let it continue. Normalcy was a shield.

I crouched briefly near Sadie, running a hand along her neck as if just checking for burrs.

"You did well," I murmured under my breath.

Her ears flicked.

Nathan drifted closer, voice casual. "Everything okay?"

"For now," I said softly. "Stay inside. No wandering. If you need something, you ask."

His jaw tightened—but he nodded.

His mother called from the kitchen. "Lunch later?"

Nathan smiled. "Smells like you're already planning it."

She laughed. "Of course I am."

I took a position near the front window, body angled so I could see reflections without standing directly in view. Nathan's father settled near the back, shotgun no longer visible but close enough to reach.

The house resumed its rhythm.

Talking. Clinking dishes. Low laughter. From the outside, nothing had changed. From the inside, everything had. Whoever had been out there hadn't wanted confrontation. They'd wanted confirmation.

And now they had it. I wasn't leaving this house again without deciding when—and how—the next move happened.

My phone vibrated once.

I didn't look at it immediately.

I waited until Nathan's mother laughed at something Marcus said, until the sound filled the room just enough to cover a breath.

Then I glanced down.

BILL: *Drone picked up thermal ghosts along the north tree line. Three positions. Recently occupied. No heat now.*

I felt the confirmation settle into place.

Not a stumble. Not a lost hiker. Not curiosity.

Placement.

They'd chosen their angles. Measured sightlines. Stayed long enough to be sure—then disappeared.

I typed back without looking down.

ME: *Copy. Maintain high and wide. No approach unless they reappear.*

The phone went dark again in my hand.

From the kitchen, Nathan's mother called out, "Coffee is still hot if anyone wants more."

I didn't move.

Three positions meant three sets of eyes.

And someone patient enough to wait.

I heard the latch.

The soft click of the screen door was wrong—not loud enough to announce itself, not quiet enough to ignore. By the time my head turned, it was already too late.

Nathan's mother was outside.

She moved with the ease of routine, unaware, stepping into the small garden just off the back of the house—no more than six yards from the siding. Lettuce. Tomatoes. Cucumbers. Familiar motions. Safe ones.

My pulse spiked.

Nathan's father saw her at the same moment I did.

He didn't shout.

He scrambled out the door instead, shotgun already in his hands, body angling instinctively to give her cover without alarming her. He stayed between her and the tree line, eyes scanning, shoulders squared.

She glanced back at him, smiling.

Then she saw the gun.

Her smile faltered, confusion flickering into worry.

He motioned urgently—flat palm, sharp pull back toward the house.

Now.

She straightened slowly, careful not to panic, and turned to come back. Each step was deliberate. Controlled.

Almost enough.

Her foot caught on a clod of mud at the edge of the garden.

She stumbled forward—

—and the world snapped tight.

A wire sang.

Thin. Metallic. Wrong.

"DOWN—!" I shouted.

She hit the ground as the shot cracked through the air.

The round didn't come for her.

It took the power line instead.

Sparks exploded overhead as the cable snapped, the report echoing sharp and final, and the house dropped into darkness all at once—lights dead, hum gone, silence roaring in its place.

The power was the target and we might have been next.

Nathan's mother crawled.

Not panicked—determined. Low to the ground, elbows and knees driving her forward while Nathan's father stayed between her and the tree line, shotgun tracking slow arcs, daring anything out there to move.

I covered the rear, eyes locked on shadow and shimmer.

She reached the house. Hands grabbed her. Pulled her inside.

The door shut. Locked.

Shades came down—not all at once, but carefully, one by one, hands steady despite the adrenaline. Every exterior door was secured. Every interior light stayed off.

The house moved into emergency rhythm.

The security team gathered gear without speaking—packs on, weapons checked, plates adjusted. Everyone packed fast and light. Essentials only. No debate.

My eyes never stopped moving.

"Bill," I murmured into my radio. "Shot confirmed. Power line hit. We're exfiling."

His voice came back calm and immediate. "Copy. Drone holding steady. High circle. No new heat signatures."

Good.

Outside, the team moved low, almost crawling, using the house as cover as they brought the vehicles around to the back porch. Tires barely crunched. Doors opened just enough. Positions were taken.

Three vehicles. All armored. All ready.

Hailey and Marcus were moved first—Vehicle Two. Quick, clean, heads down.

Nathan turned back for his parents and Sadie.

"Come on, girl," he whispered urgently, hand outstretched.

Sadie didn't hesitate.

She bolted.

Straight past us. Straight into the yard.

Not running away.

Running *toward*.

To where her family had been threatened.

"Sadie—!" Nathan hissed, panic breaking through his control.

Nathan's mother cried out once. His father reached for the door.

I shook my head sharply.

"No time," I said. It was the hardest sentence I'd spoken all day.

We couldn't call her back. We couldn't go after her. Whoever had set that wire wanted movement. Wanted chaos.

We had to deny them both.

Nathan looked like something had split open in him—but he nodded. Once.

We moved.

I pulled him into Vehicle Three with me as the doors sealed shut, heavy and final. The engines rolled low, controlled, and then we were gone—down the drive, out through cover, disappearing into the trees.

Behind us, the farmhouse vanished.

And Sadie stayed.

Nathan stared out the window, jaw locked, eyes burning. I didn't touch him. There are moments you don't interrupt.

His parents' vehicle broke off north, exactly as planned.

"Five miles," his father's voice crackled over the radio. "Daniel's place."

I exhaled when I heard the name.

Daniel wasn't just family.

He was prepared.

"Don't worry about us," his father added. "Daniel's got an underground bunker. Weapons. Ammo. We'll be safe."

Bill came back on the line, dry and approving. "That tracks. Daniel doesn't do unprepared."

My radio coughed once as I acknowledged.

We rolled in fast, covering angles as Nathan's parents were escorted inside Daniel's place—solid walls, reinforced doors, a man who looked exactly like someone who owned both a bunker and too many opinions.

Quick hugs. No lingering.

Then the doors shut.

And we turned back toward the city.

The convoy tightened formation, engines steady, speed controlled.

Behind us, the family was hidden.

Ahead of us, answers waited.

And somewhere between the two, a line had been crossed.

Nathan's POV

The road blurred past without ceremony.

No stops. No lights. No second chances.

I checked my phone again even though I already knew the answer.

"Dad?"

His voice came through steady. Controlled. Too controlled.

"We're inside," he said. "Daniel's place is sealed. Bunker's stocked. Cameras up. No one's getting near us without permission—or regret."

I swallowed.

Mom leaned into the call. "We're fine, sweetheart. Truly. You worry too much."

I almost laughed at that. Almost.

"And Sadie?" I asked.

A pause.

"We haven't seen her," Dad said carefully. "But if anyone could disappear and survive, it'd be that dog."

I closed my eyes. "I'm sorry," I said. "I brought this to your doorstep."

"No," Dad replied immediately. "You didn't. Someone else did. And we're still standing."

Daniel's voice cut in, gravelly and unbothered. "House is locked down, kid. I've got enough hardware here to make a small country uncomfortable. You focus on what you need to do."

"Thank you," I said quietly.

The call ended.

I stared out the window, jaw tight, chest burning with something that had nowhere to go.

They hadn't just threatened *me*.

They'd come for my parents.

"That was recon," Gabriel said beside me, voice low, even. "Not execution."

"That doesn't make it better," I snapped before I could stop myself.

He didn't react. Didn't correct me.

"They crossed a line," I continued. "My family could've been killed."

Gabriel nodded once. "I know."

Silence stretched between us, dense but not distant.

"They won't get another chance," he said finally. Not a promise. A fact.

The city rose up around us soon after—glass, concrete, anonymity. The convoy slipped back into traffic as though it had never left.

No one followed.

No one tried.

That almost made it worse.

We didn't all go back to the same place.

That was the point.

The convoy divided two blocks from the complex, clean and deliberate. No lingering. No hesitation.

Hailey and Marcus were taken first.

Their apartment building wasn't flashy, but it was solid— controlled access, limited sightlines, security already staged outside in plain clothes. They didn't look like guards. They looked like people waiting for rides that never came.

Hailey turned in her seat and caught my eye through the glass before the door shut.

"You don't get to disappear," she said firmly. "Not after today."

"I won't," I promised.

Marcus gave a short nod. "Bring this to an end," he said. "And text. Frequently."

The door closed. Locks engaged. They were inside—protected, watched, contained.

I exhaled only when the vehicle pulled away.

Bill's voice came through the comms. "They're set. Eyes on every entrance. Rotation already planned."

"Good," Gabriel replied.

Our vehicle didn't slow down.

We cut back toward the restaurant instead.

The city felt different now—sharper. Louder. Like it knew something had shifted and was pretending not to care. Traffic swallowed us whole, anonymity wrapping around the car like camouflage.

"You sure about this?" I asked quietly.

Bill didn't look at me. "It's the safest place right now," he said. "Controlled access. Trusted staff. We even own the cameras, and it sends a message."

"What message?" I asked.

Gabriel answered. "That we're not hiding," he said. "We're repositioning."

The restaurant came into view—lights on, exterior calm, nothing to suggest what had already bled beneath its surface.

We entered through the back.

The door shut behind us, heavy and final.

For the first time since leaving the farmhouse, I felt it settle in my chest—not relief, not fear.

Resolve.

They had tested the perimeter.

Now we were back on ours.

And whatever came next wouldn't reach my family again.

Not ever.

(28) The Longest Day

Sunlight hit my face like an accusation I didn't deserve.

We'd slept—well, *I* tried to sleep—down in the underground shelter beneath Sogno Toscano. Safe, secure, paranoid. Bill snored like a malfunctioning engine. Gabriel barely slept at all.

By morning, Gabriel escorted me back to my apartment while the staff quietly reset the front of the restaurant to look "closed for maintenance." No one questioned it; no one suspected anything. And no one but us knew what we were preparing for.

Now, I was back in my demolished apartment, broom in hand, dust in my hair, and a microphone taped under my shirt like I was starring in my own undercover episode of Dateline.

"Tell me again," I muttered to the empty air, "why does 'the bait' have to be the one who cleans up messes?"

Gabriel's voice crackled gently through my ear. "Because it has to look lived in, Nathan. Calvin expects vulnerability, not a crime scene."

"Yeah, well, could someone at least bring me a Starbucks?" I groaned.

Bill barked a laugh. "From badass to *pamper your ass*, Nathan jumps genres without warning."

I smirked. "Careful, Bill. I've shot a man in the kneecaps. Twice. And, once in the twig and berries."

"Yeah," he chuckled, "but that was yesterday. Today you're folding socks."

I picked up a torn shirt and sighed dramatically.

"I'm surrounded by children."

"Only the finest," Gabriel murmured, warm amusement threading his voice.

"Oh don't get me started with you," I muttered, cheeks warming. "I'm trying not to flirt with you on an open mic. I have to protect the virgin ears in the room."

Bill hooted so loudly the sound cracked in my ear. "Oh my God—Gabe, marry this one."

I blushed so hard I felt it in my toes.

Hours dragged.

I swept. I straightened. I threw out the junk that couldn't be salvaged. I rearranged what was still usable.

It was empty work. Quiet work. The kind of work that leaves too much room for worry.

By late morning, I chewed on my lip until it hurt.

By mid-afternoon, I'd reorganized the same shelf three times.

By early evening, loneliness settled into my bones like cold water.

"Any updates?" I whispered.

"No movement," Gabriel said. His voice was calm, but I could hear the strain underneath. "No calls. No sightings. Calvin's quiet."

"Which is bad," Bill added. "He's waiting for something."

I sat on the ruined couch, hugging a pillow with stuffing poking out.

"I hate this," I whispered. "The waiting."

Gabriel's voice softened. "I know."

I closed my eyes.

"I miss you."

A quiet breath. A soft response.

"I miss you too."

My heart tried to melt into the floor.

I stood and paced to the kitchen for something to drink. Instead of a drink, the only thing I found was more anxiety.

The sun dipped. The sky darkened. The apartment felt smaller.

Then—

BOOM.

My entire building trembled as if something massive had slammed into the Earth miles away. The windows shook. A shockwave rolled through the walls.

I dropped to my knees, hands over my head.

"What was THAT?!" I screamed.

Bill's voice blasted into the mic. "REPORT! Nathan—what direction did the sound come from?"

I scrambled to the window, palms sweating. Smoke. Orange light. Fire spiraling into the night sky in the distance.

My breath shattered in my throat.

"Oh my God…" I gasped. "Oh my GOD—GABRIEL—it's— it's the restaurant!"

Silence. Sharp. Deadly.

Then Gabriel's voice came through—stern, controlled, but shaking.

"Nathan. Listen to me carefully. No one was inside."

I froze.

"I closed it down for the entire day," he continued. "Not a single staff member. Not even Lopez… if he was foolish enough to go back."

"But the building—it's gone—it's burning—" My voice cracked.

"I know," he said. "I knew Calvin would strike something symbolic. Something important to me."

Bill growled through the speaker. "Jesus, Gabe… your whole kitchen line… your wine cellar—"

"Material," Gabriel cut in sharply. "Replaceable."

His voice softened. "You're not."

That landed like a punch to my chest.

I turned from the window, unable to look at the burning sky anymore.

"Gabe…" I whispered. "I'm so sorry."

"You have nothing to apologize for," he said, voice fierce and gentle all at once. "Nothing. He thinks he hurt me tonight. He has no idea how wrong he is."

Then something shifted in my apartment. Not loud. Not dramatic.

Just a soft, almost polite sound.

Click.

My door.

My blood froze.

"Gabriel," I whispered, "someone's in the hallway."

Bill's voice sharpened instantly. "Nathan. Stay behind cover. Now."

I backed up slowly, pulse thundering.

The doorknob twitched.

Just once.

Just enough to tell me the waiting was over.

"Gabriel…" I breathed into the mic. "I think he's here."

(29) Tick, Tick, Terror

The moment the doorknob twitched, my whole body snapped into instinct.

I vaulted over a mound of clothes like a terrified gazelle with a death wish, skidding across the floorboards and diving into my bedroom. My hands shook uncontrollably as I reached under the bed and grabbed the only "weapon" I had left — my childhood hockey stick.

A freaking hockey stick.

"Really?" I whispered to myself. "This is it? This is my John Wick moment?"

But Bill had taken the gun after my little Lopez-knee demolition, so a stick would have to do. Not ideal, but desperate people make desperate choices.

I pressed my back to the wall, stick raised like a samurai blade, breath caught in my throat. My heart thumped so hard it echoed through the wood of the stick. Every horror movie I'd ever seen suddenly seemed like a training montage.

Michael Myers, watch out — I'm the final girl tonight.

Silence. A shuffling sound.

He was inside my apartment.

Inside.

My muscles locked. My pulse roared in my ears. The air felt electric.

He was coming toward the bedroom door. Coming slowly. Deliberately.

This was it. Go time. Fight, not flight.

I inhaled sharply and coiled to strike.

One... two... three—

I whipped the door open, raised the stick over my head, and screamed bloody murder as I lunged—

Then froze mid-swing.

"—MARCUS?!"

He stood in the doorway drenched in some kind of chemical sludge, eyes red and streaming, coughing violently, his entire body trembling. And strapped to his chest — oh God —

A vest. Blocky. Wired. Covered with blinking LEDs.

The word **C-4** was printed in bold across it.

My hockey stick clattered to the floor.

"Marcus—Marcus—oh my God—are you okay?!" My voice cracked into pure panic. "Gabriel, BILL, Marcus has a bomb—GET OUT OF THE BUILDING AND CALL THE BOMB SQUAD!"

Marcus tried to speak but choked on the fumes clouding around him. His right hand trembled violently as he lifted something toward me — an old-school flip phone taped and rubber-banded to a sheet of paper. Barely clinging to it.

I tore it gently from his fingers.

Smoke or chemical vapor wafted from Marcus's clothes, burning my nose and eyes. I grabbed a towel and wiped his face, trying to keep him conscious.

"Stay with me," I pleaded. "Stay with me, buddy. I'm right here."

Then I looked down at the note.

Barely readable. Smudged. But unmistakable.

"No doubt Marcus will die if you don't act quickly, but linger too long poor Hailey dies click, click, click."

"A riddle?!" I shrieked at the universe. "SERIOUSLY?!"

Marcus whimpered, sagging to the floor.

"Hold on," I whispered, squeezing his hand. "You're gonna be okay. I promise. Just hang on to my voice."

The phone screen blinked awake — a massive analog-style CLOCK face ticking loudly.

Click. Click. Click.

"A clock…" I whispered. "He's pointing to the click… where's the clock—where's the WALL CLOCK?!"

I spun around the destroyed living room. The clock that was always hanging above the kitchen counter. Missing.

My panic skyrocketed.

"Nathan, what's happening?" Gabriel demanded through the mic. "Talk to me."

"I CAN'T FIND THE CLOCK!" I yelled, overturning cushions and boxes. "IT'S MISSING AND THE PHONE IS COUNTING DOWN!"

Marcus gagged, coughing hard.

Then— Through the thick fumes— He forced out one single word.

"Sh… shower…"

My breath caught.

"Shower?" I repeated, kneeling beside Marcus. His eyes clenched shut from the burning fumes, but he managed a weak, desperate nod.

"Okay—okay, shower. I got it." I squeezed his shoulder. "Just hold on. I'll fix this. I promise."

I scrambled to my feet and sprinted down the hall.

And that's when I heard it— first a single siren wailing somewhere in the distance… then another… and another… until the world outside erupted in a full blitz of emergency response.

Fire trucks. Ambulances. Police cruisers. Rescue vans.

They were all converging on my building— screaming through the streets with lights blazing like a second sunrise.

For half a second, hope flickered in my chest.

They're here. I'm not alone.

But hope didn't last long.

I burst into the bathroom— and froze, gasping.

There, mounted where the showerhead should've been, was my kitchen clock. Wired. Taped. Wrong.

A note dangled from the bottom edge:

pull me

"Oh God…" I whispered, heart rattling in my ribs. "If this kills me, I'm haunting EVERYONE."

I reached out. Pulled.

FWOOOOSH!

A string of polaroids burst out of the back of the clock— fluttering down like grotesque confetti, linking one to the next, spilling into a long, horrifying chain.

They shaped themselves into a body.

Hailey's body.

Her face gagged. Her wrists were bound. Her posture slumped in terror. Image after image, taped together, forming a dangling effigy with the clock as the head.

My stomach heaved. My mind snapped.

And then—

FLASH.

A retro Polaroid camera hidden high in the corner went off, a blinding burst of white.

A new photograph spat out of the machine, drifting lazily through the steam and chemical haze.

I caught it with trembling fingers.

As the image developed, everything inside me shattered.

It was me— standing exactly where I stood now— caught mid-horror.

And Hailey— real, alive, tied to a chair— trapped in some unknown location behind me in the blurred background.

Between us was a handwritten message:

"She's Next."

My scream tore through the entire apartment.

"GABRIEL—HE HAS HAILEY!"

(30) Bloodline in the Polaroids

Gabriel didn't come into the room — He *exploded* into it.

One second I was staring at the nightmare image of Hailey's polaroid body dangling from the showerhead, The next thing I knew, Gabriel was at my side, his hands flying to Marcus as Bill pulled him away, shouting orders.

Then Gabriel turned, saw the photo in my hand, saw the chain of polaroids, saw the sick display—

And his entire body jolted.

He pressed both hands to his face.

"Oh my God," he breathed. "What the hell… what the hell is he doing?"

He wasn't asking me. He wasn't asking anyone. He was asking the universe why a monster like Calvin ever crawled back into his life.

Tears burned my eyes.

"I know *exactly* what he's doing," I growled, voice cracking through rage. "He's messing with the wrong people."

My fists trembled. My veins burned. Everything inside me twisted into fury.

"I'm going to kill him."

The words tore out of me like wildfire.

My whole body seized — muscles tensing, throat tight, breath shaking.

Then the scream came up from somewhere deep, somewhere primal. A roar of anguish, terror, rage, and heartbreak combined.

"AAAHHHHH!"

Gabriel grabbed me at the peak of it. He pulled me into him, full-force, arms wrapping around my shoulders, grounding me before I shattered.

He held me while I sobbed against his chest, while I trembled, while I tried to breathe.

He didn't hush me. He didn't try to fix it.

He just held me. Hard. Firm. Safe.

When I finally steadied, he released me just enough to look into my eyes.

Then he pulled out his phone and dialed without hesitation.

"Mr. Emerson," Gabriel said, voice clean and commanding, "we have a situation. I need you at Nathan's apartment immediately. Take him to the safehouse. I'm leaving Marcus with Bill and emergency services."

He paused.

"And Emerson—gather these disturbing polaroids. Take the clock. I need your expertise in the analysis of these items. We must locate his friend Hailey, and based on your history, you're the only one who can do it. Move. Quickly. NOW."

He hung up.

Something clicked inside me. Not logic. Not memory.

Instinct.

The chair in the background. Hailey strapped to it. The legs. The wood. The pattern.

I'd seen it before.

I grabbed Gabriel's sleeve. "Wait—wait—I think I know that chair."

He turned sharply.

"What chair?"

"The one Hailey's tied to," I said, head throbbing. "I've seen it. I KNOW I've seen it."

I squeezed my eyes shut. The headache split behind my temples.

"Nathan?" Gabriel cupped my jaw, worry lacing his voice. "What is it? What are you remembering?"

"It… hurts," I muttered, pressing a hand to my forehead. "Everything hurts. My brain is fried."

"So many emotions," he whispered. "Terrors you shouldn't have to face."

He hugged me again — briefly — grounding me.

Then like lightning in my skull— I had an epiphany. My eyes flew open.

"That chair…" I whispered. "Oh God. Gabriel — that chair is from my parents' house."

Gabriel froze.

"My parents' house," I repeated, terror swelling inside me. "We were just there not long ago. He has Hailey THERE. And— maybe—maybe he has my parents too? So, he must have followed them to Daniel's house to collect my folks! Which means…Daniel's either dead or on his side…"

The horror in my chest became a scream trapped behind my ribs.

Gabriel didn't waste a second.

He snatched up his phone so fast it nearly split in half.

"Emerson," he barked the moment the call connected. "New plan. You're still coming here—but only to collect the materials. I'm taking Nathan directly to his parents' home. Send a full security team ahead of us. They are to set up a perimeter and lockdown until I arrive with Nathan. No one enters the house. NO ONE. Understood?"

He ended the call without waiting for a response.

We moved.

Police were evacuating the entire building. Fire crews and paramedics swarmed every floor. The bomb squad hauled

Marcus out on a stretcher, the vest removed, his shirt shredded, chemical burns all over his arms.

My heart was breaking watching him.

"Marcus—" I whispered.

Gabriel squeezed my shoulder. "Two of my men are going with him. He's in good hands."

Then the air thundered above us.

A helicopter. One of Gabriel's.

A tactical team guided us through the chaos toward the barricaded street. On the second-floor landing, I spotted Mr. Emerson stepping into the hallway, flashing credentials at the police, already slipping past the line of responders without resistance.

"Emerson's highly regarded here," Gabriel said as we ran. "He'll get what he needs."

The helicopter landed hard on the asphalt, rotors kicking up dust and flashing red lights from every direction.

Gabriel ushered me inside, his hand on my back, guiding me like precious cargo.

"Pilot, take us up," he ordered. "NOW!"

The helicopter lifted just as Marcus's ambulance peeled away below us with sirens howling.

My apartment building shrank beneath us. Mr. Emerson emerged carrying the materials Gabriel told him to gather. The city lights blurred.

Gabriel leaned close, voice steady, warm, fierce.

"We're going to your parents' house, Nathan. And we're going to bring Hailey back."

His hand found mine.

"You're not doing this alone."

(31) The Moffett House Now No Heartbeat

The moment the helicopter touched down on the wide sweep of lush green yard, the place felt wrong. Not dangerous. Not chaotic. Wrong.

Too quiet. Too still. Like a stage set before the actors enter.

My childhood home sat at the end of its long winding gravel driveway exactly as it always had—a small two-story farmhouse with white siding, a weathered front porch, and a shed standing sentinel at the turn-in where cars parked.

And Mom and Dad's cars were parked right where they should be. Perfectly normal. Perfectly staged.

We stepped out of the helicopter into the warm scent of dirt and cedar, security agents forming a tight ring around us as Gabriel led the way toward the house.

"The back door is usually unlocked," I whispered, pointing. "It opens straight into the kitchen."

Gabriel nodded but didn't deviate from protocol. We crouched beside the shed, gravel crunching softly under our boots.

"Thermals," Gabriel ordered.

A voice crackled in his earpiece immediately.

"We've scanned multiple times, sir. No bodies. No heat signatures. Not inside the house, not in the barn, not in the machine shed. Sweep completed thirty seconds before touchdown."

"Nothing?" Gabriel repeated, tense.

"Negative. It's clean. Unless someone's wearing a thermal-blocking suit or a stop-movement reflector suit that bounces heat detection."

My stomach twisted.

They didn't know about the old stone-lined cellar dug deep beneath the house. Dad always joked it was "as old as the earth itself"—cold, silent, perfect for storing potatoes. Or hiding someone.

A shiver crawled up my spine.

Then— CLICK.

The back floodlights snapped on.

White light sliced through the darkness, illuminating the grassy yard and— a barn cat.

A skinny, half-wild tabby jumped back from the sudden brightness, tail puffed, startled by its own shadow.

But I didn't get a chance to laugh.

Instantly, a dozen tiny red laser dots flicked onto the cat's fur. Sniper sights.

The cat froze.

Then one by one, the red lights blinked off as the shooters reset.

Gabriel hissed quietly, "Hold fire! Everyone hold fire!"

My heart hammered.

And that's when I saw it.

Movement in the window. High up. Fast. A shadow pulling back from the glass.

"Up in the window!" I choked out. "Someone was just looking out!"

Gabriel snapped toward me. "Did you recognize them?"

I shook my head. "Too quick. Just a silhouette."

His expression hardened.

"Alpha, move to the south side," Gabriel commanded into his mic. "Slow approach. Eyes up. No sudden entries."

I clutched his forearm without meaning to. He looked down, saw the tremor in my hand, and squeezed back—firm, reassuring.

I wasn't allowed to call my parents since our initial hang-up after they were "safe" at Daniel's place. I didn't know if they were alive, or tied up, or lying cold on the floor somewhere inside. And Hailey—sweet, loud, chaotic Hailey—was God knows where.

I couldn't breathe.

"Bravo team," Gabriel continued, "take the north entrance. No radio chatter, no sound. Move silently."

Shapes slipped into the shadows, disappearing around the farmhouse.

"Charlie team," he said, lowering his voice, "you're with us. East flank behind the trees. Delta team—cover six and nine."

Agents peeled off like ghosts. Boots softened in the grass. Silhouettes dissolved into moonlit shadows.

The farmhouse loomed ahead, innocent in the beams of the floodlights. Too innocent.

Gabriel pulled me close, voice low in my ear.

"We're going to get Hailey," he whispered. "And your parents. But if Calvin is in there waiting… we approach this with precision."

"I know," I whispered, but my voice cracked. "I just… I can't lose anyone else."

"You won't," he said fiercely.

Then— From somewhere beneath the house— A sound echoed through the ground.

A deep, hollow thud. Once. Twice. Then silence.

Gabriel stiffened.

I froze.

He whispered, "Nathan… was that…?"

I swallowed hard.

"That sounded like the cellar door."

The moon hung high and ruthless, its pale light spilling into the cellar through the open bulkhead doors. The glow hit the stone floor first—a smooth, worn slab Dad always joked was "older than the Civil War and twice as stubborn."

Tonight, it looked like an altar.

Beyond that glimmer of moonlight, the shadows thickened. Not empty. Not harmless—occupied.

I saw it before the team even spoke: A chair leg. A shoe tip. A hint of movement.

Then the muffled cries reached us—faint, shaky, terrified.

"Alpha team, report," Gabriel commanded, voice taut as a wire.

The team leader raised a fist and approached the cellar entrance with surgical precision. They'd already swept the bulkhead for tripwires and explosives. They wouldn't risk opening it until certain.

But that thud we heard earlier? That was the doors thrown wide, slamming against the stone. An invitation from Calvin. Or a clock strike. Either way, it made my skin crawl.

Two agents crouched, rifles angled low, and peered into the darkness.

"Slight movement confirmed," Alpha leader muttered. "I see… three figures. Tied to chairs. Gagged. All upright."

My heart stopped.

"Describe them," Gabriel said.

"Two appear older—approximately sixties. Male and female. The third is… younger. Female. Early twenties. Possibly the roommate mentioned. In the center there appears to be a deceased dog."

"Hailey and Sadie!" I whispered hoarsely.

My knees nearly buckled.

Gabriel steadied me by the elbow without looking away from the cellar.

"Proceed," he ordered.

The tactical team descended the steep steps silently, flashlights cutting tight beams through the dark. Shadows clung to the walls. Dust swirled like frightened ghosts.

Mom. Dad. Hailey.

All three sat in straight-back wooden chairs, wrists tied, ankles bound, heads jerking up at the approach. Their eyes were red from crying, wide with fear—and frantic with urgency.

They weren't just scared.

They were trying to warn us.

"Hostages located and conscious, dog deceased—named Sadie per collar," Alpha confirmed. "No visible bombs or wiring. They're attempting to communicate—" He paused. "Can't make out the words. Permission to ungag?"

Gabriel raised his mic to his mouth— when Hailey suddenly lurched forward, thrashing against her restraints so hard the chair legs scraped the floor.

A muffled, frantic scream ripped from behind her gag.

Then Mom jerked the same way. Followed by Dad.

All three were shaking their heads violently, eyes wide, desperate.

They weren't pleading for rescue.

They were trying to stop us.

The team leader tensed.

"Sir—they're signaling hard. Resisting entry. Trying to warn—"

Hailey screamed again, muffled but piercing.

Dad stomped his heel into the floor—sharp, deliberate.

Short-short-short… long-long-long… short-short-short…

The pattern repeated, urgent.

Mom shook her head harder, eyes locked on the door.

My blood went cold.

Gabriel froze, listening.

Short-short-short… long-long-long… short-short-short…

"N… O…" he said low.

Then the next set—faster, insistent.

Short-short… long-short-long… long-long-long… short…

Bill's voice cut in. "They're not mumbling 'no bomb.' They're warning us 'NO! BOMB!'—warning of explosives."

I felt the air leave my lungs.

Dad wasn't saying it was safe. He was screaming danger.

"They're telling us there's a bomb," I whispered, voice shaking. "It's not clear—it's rigged."

Gabriel's jaw locked.

"Hold," he ordered instantly. "Possible remote sensor. Sweep for devices—non-entry protocol."

The team shifted outside—tools out, scanners active.

Dad stomped again—same pattern, frantic.

NO! BOMB!

Mom's eyes pleaded.

Hailey thrashed.

They'd been trying to save us from walking straight into it.

Calvin hadn't just taken them.

He'd turned the room into a trap and we'd almost sprung it. Calvin wasn't finished.

And whatever came next… was already in play.

"Wait—stop!" I hissed, grabbing Gabriel's arm before he could give Alpha permission. "Remember the clue—click, click, click. And the clock!"

Gabriel's eyes narrowed as he replayed it.

"And Hailey's 'head' in the shower," I added. "It was the clock. The clue wasn't just about time. It was about mechanics. Something—something dangerous."

Just then, a soft illumination glowed from Gabriel's pocket—his phone buzzing.

Mr. Emerson.

Gabriel answered instantly, stepping back into shadow.

"Emerson."

The voice on the line was brisk, tight, edged with controlled alarm.

"Mr. Michaels," Emerson said.

Hearing Gabriel's last name jolted me. Gabriel Michaels. And damn, somehow it suited him even more in a crisis.

Emerson continued quickly:

"I've examined the clock and the polaroids of the female hostage. The arrangement wasn't random. There are three distinct garments overlapping in the images, suggesting he's referencing three pending detonations. That ties directly to his 'click, click, click' clue."

My stomach bottomed out.

"More importantly," Emerson went on, "the polaroids were attached with cherry blossom bomb-shaped stickers. Those are a calling card used in underground weapons markets to mark Ying-Tao grenades."

Gabriel's posture stiffened.

Emerson's voice sharpened:

"If there are victims, and there probably are, and those victims are gagged, DO NOT—under ANY circumstances—remove the gags. I repeat: do not ungag them. Calvin has most likely inserted Ying-Tao grenades into the victims' mouths. Removing the gag will dislodge the safety tension and trigger detonation."

A cold wave shot down my spine.

If Alpha team had pulled the gags a moment ago—Hailey, my mom, my dad—would've been obliterated. And anyone standing within yards of them too.

Gabriel didn't hesitate.

He snapped to his radio.

"Alpha, stand down. Do NOT touch the hostages. The gags remain ON. Back away five yards and maintain visual."

His voice was iron—unshakeable, commanding, deadly clear.

Alpha immediately echoed back:

"Standing down, stepping away. Hostages secure. No contact."

But Emerson wasn't done.

"Mr. Michaels!" Emerson's voice rose sharply. "There's more!"

Gabriel pressed the phone harder to his ear.

"Yes?"

"The Ying-Tao grenades have dual-trigger capability. The first trigger is gag removal. The second is a remote detonation switch. Calvin can set them off anywhere within a two-mile radius."

My knees nearly gave out.

Gabriel's eyes flashed—something between fury and a depth of fear I'd never seen in him.

That was all he needed. He snapped into action.

"Alpha stays with the hostages," Gabriel ordered. "No touching. No noise. No sudden movements."

Then to the rest:

"Bravo team, Charlie team—break off and sweep the perimeter. Check every inch of pasture, barn, shed, silo, and a machine bay. I want Calvin found."

He motioned with a firm gesture, directing the split of forces.

The Delta team moved into tight formation behind us, shielding both Gabriel and me with a diamond pattern used for high-value targets.

The night air thickened around us. Somewhere out there in the dark— Calvin was watching.

We moved back toward the open yard, where the grass swayed in the moonlight and the house stood silent as a tomb.

Then— Gabriel's phone rang again.

Shrill. Urgent. Cutting straight through the chill.

He stared at the caller ID.

His jaw locked.

He answered.

"Go."

(32) Two Calls, Someone Dies

Two calls came in at once. Gabriel's screen lit up with **Calvin**. The other call came in with **Bill Goldberg**.

Gabriel hesitated—just for a breath. I could see it: the urge to grab both calls at once. But reality didn't allow that.

He declined Bill's call with a swipe, jaw tightening, and answered the monster.

"Calvin?" Gabriel said tersely, already pacing. "I assume it's you. What do you want?"

His tone was ice—controlled, lethal.

He snapped his fingers at me, motioning sharply: *Phone. Now.*

I fumbled to unlock it, palms sweating. Gabriel snatched it the instant it lit, fingers flying over the screen like stabbing motions. He couldn't talk to Bill directly, not while Calvin was on the line—but he could text him from *my* phone.

For a second I saw the message he typed:

"WHAT DID MARCUS SAY?"

He hit send. Then he stepped away from me—just a small step, but enough to shield the screen from my eyes.

Calvin's voice on the other end was a sickly purr, echoing in Gabriel's ear. I couldn't hear the words, but I could *feel* the venom. Gabriel's shoulders tensed with every syllable.

Then, Bill's reply came through.

Gabriel froze.

He stared at the screen.

His face went pale.

And then he turned toward me.

A single tear broke free from his left eye and fell fast, like it couldn't stay attached to him under the weight of what he'd read.

His lips shaped soundlessly:

"I'm sorry, Nathan."

He handed my phone back into my shaking hands.

I looked down.

The message burned straight through me:

"Marcus is dead, Gabe. Died from all the trauma he suffered. While he was choking up blood, he managed two garbled words: 'Neighbor's house.'"

My body responded before my brain did.

My knees gave out.

The phone slipped from my fingers and hit the grass with a dull thud.

A member of the security team lunged and caught me under the arms, holding me upright as the sobs tore out of me. I pressed my face into the vest of a stranger while the world behind my eyelids shattered.

Marcus. Sweet, funny, bright Marcus. Drenched in chemicals, wired with explosives, terrified out of his mind— and now gone.

Because of Calvin.

Because he wanted me.

Because he wanted Gabriel to suffer.

The grief ripped through me like a serrated blade. I couldn't holler—my voice collapsed inward. Hot, muffled, strangled sobs soaked into the guard's vest while I shook and shook.

My friend. My friend was dead.

And a murderer was listening in on the other line.

From somewhere above the storm in my head, I heard Gabriel's voice—low, hollow, vibrating with a wrath I had never heard from him before.

"Is that what you really want, Calvin?" Gabriel said into the phone. His tone wasn't angry.

It was *ancient*.

A warning from a man with nothing left to lose.

Calvin must have heard the crack in my breath, the way I broke against the guard's vest. Even through the phone's distant speaker, even through my clenched teeth pressing back sobs, he *heard* it.

And he reveled in it.

Gabriel's jaw flexed sharply at the sound of Calvin's next words—slithering through the speaker with smugness dripping off every syllable.

"Ah… another casualty. Marcus. Such a small price for the debt you owe me, Gabriel. You should be thanking me. I'm simply returning the interest you accrued with your betrayal."

Gabriel went utterly still.

Then he spoke, voice low and steady—steady in that terrifying way a blade stays steady right before it slices.

"Betrayal?" he repeated slowly. "Is that the word you've settled on, Calvin?"

He didn't shout. He didn't tremble. He didn't even raise his tone.

It was the calm in a man who had finally decided something fundamental.

Gabriel stepped away by a few paces, hand clenched around the phone, and his voice unfurled—quiet, lethal, and sharp as broken glass.

"Listen to me, Calvin.

You keep rewriting history in your head to make yourself the victim. But you and I both know the truth.

You weren't betrayed.

You were *stopped*.

Stopped from bleeding good people dry. Stopped from manipulating families into financial ruin. Stopped from turning partnerships into blackmail and loyalty into chains.

I didn't betray you, Calvin. I broke free of you. And you have never forgiven me for choosing integrity over your corruption.

Marcus didn't die because of me. You murdered him.

You strapped a bomb to an innocent man. You drenched him in chemicals. You terrorized him for sport. You used him—someone with nothing to do with our past—as a pawn in a game only you are playing.

That wasn't a message to me.

That was proof.

Proof you've descended so far into your obsession, you don't even remember what started this war.

But hear me clearly now—

This ends with me standing over you. One way or another."

Calvin was silent for a moment on the other end. A silence that said he'd been struck—wounded—but not defeated.

Then he chuckled. A chilling, soft, delighted little chuckle.

"Oh, Gabriel… You always did talk like a hero. Let's see how heroic you are when the next clock runs out."

And the line went dead.

(33) The Radius of Fear Begins The Hunt

We didn't waste a second.

The moment Calvin hung up, Gabriel snapped his fingers and Delta team tightened formation. His fury wasn't loud; it was *focused.* A bottled hurricane. The air around him vibrated like something holy and furious had been shaken awake.

"We know where he is," Gabriel said, his voice flint-hard. "Three neighbor properties. All within the two-mile radius."

I wiped the wetness from my face with the back of my hand. The grief for Marcus hadn't passed — it sat like a stone in my ribs — but something else rose over it now.

Rage.

And a clarity I'd never felt before.

"He won't get away," I whispered, more to myself than anyone else.

Gabriel heard me anyway.

His eyes slid to mine — soft for the briefest heartbeat, then steely again.

"He won't," he promised.

Just then, Gabriel's phone buzzed sharply. Mr. Emerson.

Gabriel answered. I pressed close, listening.

"Mr. Michaels," Emerson said, voice clipped and tense. "I've found something. The Ying-Tao grenades have a *secondary disable mechanism.* If you neutralize the remote trigger first, there's a thirty-second window to disarm the mouth devices."

Gabriel's brows tightened. "How?"

"They operate on a dual-sensor integrity strip. If the remote signal dies abruptly, the grenades enter a safety lag — but only for thirty seconds. During that gap, if someone can clamp the victim's jaw still and slide the tension pin forward through the gag fabric—"

"—they won't detonate," Gabriel finished.

"Correct… but only if done quickly, and in sequence. The remote must be cut off first. If the pin is touched while the remote is active, they explode instantly."

Gabriel lifted his eyes toward the dark pasture ahead.

"Understood," he said. "Send the full disable protocol to Alpha team."

"Yes, sir."

The call ended.

I exhaled shakily. "So we get the remote first. Then we disarm everyone."

Gabriel nodded once.

Then he turned to me, gripping my shoulders firmly.

"Nathan… once we find him—once Calvin is separated from his remote—stay behind me."

I didn't argue. I didn't blink. But Gabriel must've seen something in my eyes, because he softened.

"This is my fight," he said quietly. "But I know you need… something. A chance to hit him. A chance to stand up for Marcus."

My throat clenched.

"Yeah," I whispered. "I do."

He nodded slowly, deliberately.

"And you'll get it. I will give you that moment — when it's safe — when he can't trigger anything. But until then, you do everything I say. Understood?"

"Yes."

We moved.

Delta team fanned out around us as we crossed the property line and headed down the moonlit rural road. The night was thick with insects and the low hum of adrenaline. My heart beat so hard I could feel it behind my knees.

The three neighboring houses sat a mile away — spaced out like abandoned checkpoints in a horror movie.

House One: dark, lifeless, completely still House Two: faint light in the kitchen window House Three: barn lights on, but no house lights

As we approached the first intersection, the Delta leader held up a fist and everyone froze.

"Movement. Southeast quadrant."

Gabriel leaned close to me. "House Two or Three."

Then another buzz — Emerson again, text only.

REMOTE SIGNAL IS ACTIVE. STILL WITHIN RANGE. CHECK FOR INTERFERENCE PATTERN NEAR HOUSE THREE.

Gabriel's eyes flashed.

"He's at the barn," Gabriel murmured.

My lungs locked.

That barn… That damn barn where I played hide and seek as a kid whenever we visited neighbors. And now it held a monster.

"Delta," Gabriel whispered, "three-point sweep. Charlie team maintains distance at seventy meters. Bravo flank the west side."

He turned to me one last time.

"Nathan. Stay close."

I nodded.

We crept through the tall grass. The barn loomed in the dark like a sleeping creature.

My pulse hammered.

From inside the barn — faint, rhythmic tapping. Metal on wood. Tap. Tap. Tap.

"You hear that?" I whispered.

Gabriel's jaw clenched.

"It's him."

We reached the side entrance. Delta team stacked up.

One guard tested the handle with a gloved hand.

Unlocked.

That alone meant trouble.

Gabriel leaned toward my ear. "He wants us inside."

"I know."

Heavy breath. Heart pounding. A cold sweat on my spine.

Then Gabriel lifted a clenched fist.

"Three… two… one—"

The door swung open.

The barn interior glowed under a single lantern.

And there, sitting on a wooden crate, smiling like the devil himself—

Calvin Marshall.

Holding a small black remote in his hand. His thumb resting lightly on the trigger.

"Nice evening for a visit," he said calmly. "Wouldn't you agree, Gabriel?"

I tasted blood. I'd bitten the inside of my cheek without realizing.

Gabriel stepped forward.

"Calvin," he said softly, "this ends now."

Calvin clicked his tongue.

"Oh, Gabriel… everything ends when I say it ends."

He lifted the remote a fraction, letting it catch the lantern light.

Behind me, I felt Gabriel subtly extend an arm in front of me.

His message clear:

Not yet. Not until the remote is gone.

My fists trembled. My pulse shook my entire body.

But I waited.

Because we needed the right moment.

Because I needed to survive long enough to punch this bastard's teeth in.

And because Marcus deserved justice, not a martyr's grave.

Calvin's smile widened.

"Shall we begin?"

(34) The Bullet Between Us

(Nathan's POV — Love is the Last Weapon)

The barn smelled like old hay, cold air, and fear.

Calvin sat casually on that crate, legs crossed, lantern glow painting a sickly halo behind him. The black remote dangled from his fingers as if it weighed nothing. As if my friends' lives, my parents' lives, meant nothing.

"Nathan Moffett," Calvin purred when he finally laid eyes on me. "The hound from hell himself. The pathetic little spark Gabriel would risk everything for. I must admit… you're less impressive in person."

My face flushed with fury. I stepped forward.

Gabriel blocked me instantly with an outstretched arm.

"Don't," he murmured. A warning. A plea.

Calvin laughed. "Oh how loyal he is to you, Nathan. Isn't that adorable? Like a dog guarding his favorite chew toy."

"Watch your mouth," I snarled.

Calvin raised the remote a fraction. "Ah-ah-ah. Careful, puppy. You bark too loud, and I push this little button. And three darling, dear mouths will explode."

I froze.

Gabriel's entire posture shifted. Grounded. Controlled. Neither fear nor rage — just deadly focus.

"Hold it right there, Gabriel," Calvin taunted, wiggling the remote. "No sudden movements. Or I end three more lives before you take your next breath."

What Calvin didn't know — what he *couldn't* know — was that Mr. Emerson had been listening to the entire time. Invisible, tethered through Gabriel's phone signal.

Emerson, the man whose tech expertise outstripped Calvin by galaxies.

Gabriel's fingers twitched — almost imperceptibly.

Two Delta team members shifted their aim to the remote. The captain keyed in on Gabriel's hand.

And Charlie team... Charlie team's sniper had a bead on Calvin's right hand.

Timing was everything now.

A single breath could alter the outcome.

Calvin sneered. "Look at you all. Trembling. Afraid. You think this ends with you? You think you—"

Crack.

The sniper's bullet snapped the remote from Calvin's hand like it was plucked by an invisible god.

Calvin's scream was primal. His hand wasn't mangled — but it was useless, bleeding, trembling.

The remote hit the earthen floor with a dull clack.

Everything exploded into motion.

Calvin dove for it with his one good hand—

—but Emerson's device surged first.

A tiny *ping* in Gabriel's pocket meant only one thing:

REMOTE SIGNAL TERMINATED. 30-SECOND DISABLE WINDOW ACTIVE.

But Calvin didn't know that.

He scrambled for the remote—missed—then grabbed something else from beneath the crate.

A gun.

Loaded.

He turned toward me first.

The barrel stared at me like an eye of death.

For a moment, everything slowed.

My heartbeat thundered in my ears. The barn, the lantern, the men — all blurred.

I didn't care if I died.

But I would *not* let Gabriel be taken from this world.

Calvin's wrist twitched.

He moved the barrel to Gabriel.

Gabriel didn't flinch.

I did.

I saw the line. The trajectory. The timing. The madness. The love.

And my body moved before I could think.

I ran. I sprinted. I launched.

"NO!" Gabriel shouted, lunging after me.

The gun fired.

One deafening shot.

And the bullet tore into my chest midair, right as my body slammed into Gabriel, knocking him back onto the dirt floor. A burst of heat. A blossom of pain so white-hot it felt like being branded by lightning.

I heard Gabriel scream my name — raw, ragged, terrified.

Then—

Thud-thud-thud-thud-thud!

A second sniper unloaded into Calvin.

Calvin's body jerked. Then fell.

The demon was dead.

My breathing hitched. Shallow. Wet. Wrong.

Blood spread across Gabriel's hands as he held me.

His voice cracked. "Nathan—Nathan stay with me—please—look at me—God, no—"

Around us, teams surged to disarm the grenades in the cellar.

But everything in my world narrowed to one thing:

Gabriel's face above me. His tears fell hot onto my cheeks. His voice breaking.

"You saved me," he whispered.

I tried to smile.

"You'd… do it for me."

My vision blurred.

Gabriel pressed his forehead to mine.

"Don't die, Nathan. Don't you dare die on me."

(35) The Light Above the Thunder

The world came back to me in pieces.

A beep. A blur. A ceiling that didn't belong to any barn I knew. My chest felt like someone had shoved a hot brick inside it, then duct taped it into place.

Voices drifted in and out like fog rolling over a field.

"His vitals are steady—" "BP stabilizing—" "Mr. Michaels, you need to breathe—Nathan will be alright" "We saved the bullet—per your request—" "Sir, please sit, you're white as a ghost—"

My eyes cracked open.

Everything was too bright.

And then — through the brightness — I saw silhouettes.

Two. One tall, tense, unmistakably Gabriel. One smaller, trembling — Mom. Dad stood behind her, shaky but upright. And Hailey — alive, bawling into a tissue.

"Oh wow…" I croaked, voice thick as pudding. "You guys look like hell."

Everyone froze.

"Did you… Did you see the dark one himself or what?" I blinked exaggeratedly. "Was he handsome? Did he moisturize?"

Mom sobbed harder. Gabriel dropped into the chair beside me, gripping the railing like it kept him alive too.

"Nathan," he rasped. "Oh God—Nathan—"

"Are my parents okay?" I slurred, pointing vaguely at the shapes around me. "Hey Mom… Dad… do you think you'll mind if I get shot?"

Mom wailed. Dad shook his head at the ceiling. Gabriel made the strangled sound of a man about to pass out and kiss me simultaneously.

"Did you… Did you know I got shot?" I whispered conspiratorially, leaning slightly toward Gabriel. "It freakin' hurt like wiping your backside repeatedly fast with a cheese grater. I don't have firsthand experience with that, but I think you get the visual of my meaning."

Hailey snorted so loud a nurse jumped.

Gabriel covered his face with a hand.

"Nathan—"

"I don't like Calvin," I announced suddenly. "I think he and Lopez have something in common."

Gabriel blinked. "What's that?"

"Bullet holes for dickheads."

Hailey choked again. A nurse squeaked. Dad's jaw dropped. Gabriel pressed his forehead to my arm like he was praying.

"Nathan," he managed, voice breaking, "please—please stop talking about bullet holes—"

But anesthesia-me wasn't done.

"Did you know I was in emergency surgery?" I rambled, waving one limp hand. "Yeah… there was one cute doctor trying to cut in on the action."

A nurse actually *walked out of the room*, laughing silently with tears in her eyes.

Gabriel mouthed something to Heaven for strength.

"How many nurses does it take to screw in a light bulb?" I asked the room gravely.

The room fell silent.

"I don't really know," I continued. "But I know when the light came back on, they seemed to scatter away from Dr. Fisher, the hottie young doctor over there….They just scattered like cockroaches do when the light switch flicked on."

The nurses ERUPTED.

Dad made a sound like a dying owl. Gabriel sagged back in his chair, fingers dragging down his face.

"Oh my God… Nathan… please…"

"You know this medicine is pretty good," I mused aloud. "Do you think it comes in grape flavor? I like grapes a lot."

A young nurse wheezed.

Gabriel was now halfway collapsed over my blanket, laughing and crying into my arm at the same time.

I lifted my other hand and poked at my bandaged chest.

"I can feel where the bullet was before they took it out," I informed the room solemnly. "Do you think if I drink water the water will flow out of me as it does in those cartoons when someone got shot? Because that would be cool."

Gabriel looked up, eyes glassy. "Absolutely not. No. Never. Drink nothing. Ever."

I blinked at him.

"Gabriel?"

"Yes, Nathan?" he whispered, breathless.

"I think someone took off my clothes."

Gabriel froze.

"And probed me like aliens tend to do to handsome guys like me."

The room collectively *stopped breathing*.

I squinted suspiciously.

"Are you an alien, by chance, Gabriel?" I reached for him dramatically. "I'd like a probe, please."

Mom fainted. Dad swore. Hailey shriek-laughed into the wall. A nurse dropped a clipboard. Gabriel turned crimson, collapsed onto the railing, and begged the Earth to swallow him alive.

And me?

I smiled dopily, drifting back into a soft haze.

"Alien probe…" I mumbled. "Only if it's gentle like."

Everything faded again.

And the last thing I heard was Gabriel whispering against my cheek:

"You're alive. You're ridiculous. And you're mine."

(36) The Weight of Living

When I woke again, the room was quieter.

Less chaos. Less laughter. More gravity.

I could tell by the way the nurses spoke softly and the way Gabriel leaned close, elbows on his knees, head bowed like he'd been praying that whole time. His fingers were curled loosely near my hip, not quite touching, but close enough to feel the warmth he radiated.

He looked up the moment my breath hitched.

"You're awake," he whispered.

"You look…" I squinted at him. "Like you haven't slept in a week."

"Try three days," he murmured.

I blinked. "Three?"

He nodded. "You were in and out. Mostly under. Stable, but hurting. The surgeons said you're a fighter."

"They don't know the half of it," I muttered.

His eyes softened—then clouded.

The silence that followed felt heavy, swollen with the absence of someone who should have been here.

"Marcus," I whispered.

Gabriel's jaw tightened. He reached out and carefully, reverently, took my hand.

"He's gone," Gabriel said quietly. "He fought longer than they expected. He told Bill… he told all of us what he could before he went unconscious. If he hadn't… we never would've known where to find Hailey or your parents."

I swallowed down a lump that felt sharper than my bullet wound.

"I didn't get to say goodbye."

"You weren't meant to," Gabriel whispered. "He didn't want you remembering him in pain. He wanted you alive."

My throat trembled.

"And he would want this," Gabriel continued softly. "A chance to honor him. Properly."

"Yeah," I breathed. "He deserves that."

And so — we gave it to him.

(A Memorial for Marcus)

It wasn't grand. Marcus wouldn't have wanted that.

The hospital had a quiet reflection garden — stone benches, a central fountain, and a canopy of old trees that swayed like guardians. Gabriel arranged it with the hospital staff; Bill brought flowers; Hailey brought a framed picture; my parents came too.

And I— I came in a wheelchair, wrapped in a blanket I pretended wasn't Gabriel's.

We gathered around the fountain just as the sun dipped low, turning the sky warm and soft — Marcus would've joked it looked like "God's filter on Instagram."

Hailey spoke first.

"We teased him," she said, voice shaking. "About his obsession with sour candies, about his loud snoring, about the way he'd always start a story in the middle. But... he was ours. And he was *good*. The kind of good that doesn't need announcements or medals. Just... everyday kindness."

Bill cleared his throat, voice deeper and rougher than usual.

"He had guts. More than most athletes I ever worked with. And heart. The guy had real heart."

My parents nodded. Mom wiped a tear.

Gabriel stepped closer to me, placing his hand gently on my good shoulder.

"Nathan," he whispered. "This is your moment. Say what you need."

I swallowed hard.

The garden blurred.

And then I spoke.

"Marcus wasn't the kind of friend who asked for attention," I began slowly. "He was the kind who… showed up. With food when you needed cheering up. With jokes when you needed distraction. With silence when you needed company."

My breath cracked.

"He didn't deserve what happened. Not even close. But he faced it with courage. He held on long enough to save the people *I* love. He saved my life. He saved Hailey. He saved my parents. And even if he's gone… he's still here. In every good choice I make from now on. In every kindness I give. In every laugh we share."

I looked at the fountain as the water glimmered gold.

"Thank you, Marcus," I whispered. "For staying. For fighting. For being my friend."

A soft breeze lifted the leaves.

And Gabriel squeezed my shoulder gently.

We set a small bouquet of white and blue flowers on the stone edge. A simple card. Just one line:

"You mattered."

That was all Marcus ever needed.

(37) The Truth Worn on a Chain

I woke up again mid-morning, the kind of morning where sunlight feels lazy, drifting across the floor like it has nowhere urgent to be.

Gabriel was there.

Not hovering. Not pacing. Not tense.

Just sitting beside me in a soft gray chair, elbows on his knees, fingers lightly touching something hanging from his neck.

A chain.

A long, thin, silver chain.

And on it — resting against his chest — was a small, dark, metallic shape.

My bullet.

I stared at it, breath catching.

"Gabriel…?" I whispered, my voice still sanded down by surgery.

His head lifted slowly — as if each inch carried weight — and when our eyes met, something in him broke open gently, like a door that had been locked for years.

"You're awake," he breathed.

"You're… wearing my wound."

He didn't look ashamed of it. Didn't look proud either. He looked… *connected* to it. To me.

"It's the bullet that should've killed me," he said quietly. "And the one that almost killed you."

He lifted it once, just enough for me to see the dented metal's new shine from being polished.

"I had it cleaned and welded into a pendant last night," he said. "It… reminds me of what you did. And who you are."

"And who is that?" I asked, half-teasing, half-trembling.

"The man who saved my life," he said. "The man who protected me without hesitation. The man who… made me feel something I didn't think I had left in me."

My heart did its best impression of a flipped pancake.

A slow smile tugged at my lips.

"So," I murmured, "you gonna tell me your full backstory now, Mr. Mysterious Billionaire Angel-Man?"

Gabriel let out a breath that might have been a laugh, if it weren't so heavy with emotion.

He shifted closer to my bed and placed the bullet pendant gently against the blanket near my ribcage — directly over my heart.

And then he began.

"My name is Gabriel Aiden Michaels," he said softly. "I own thirty-six companies across eight sectors. I manage three international banks, a real estate empire, a security firm, and a tech conglomerate that works with government alliances on future defense systems."

He paused.

"I was the youngest partner in the National Security Safety Alliance at twenty-four. That's when I met Emerson. He was brilliant, impossible, stubborn — and honest. We formed a bond over innovation and long nights in labs most people never see."

He rubbed the bridge of his nose, memory weighing on him.

"Calvin was my employer once… and then my competitor. He saw potential in me, invested in my rise — and then tried to control it. When I refused to surrender my intellectual property, he retaliated. Hard. My first company nearly folded. My sister's fiancé was killed in the fallout. My mother had to be relocated. It was war."

"And you won," I whispered.

"In business, yes," he said. "In peace? Not even close. Calvin promised revenge. And now… here we are."

I swallowed.

"And I'm just… caught in the middle?"

Gabriel shook his head.

"No. You're the reason I survived to finish the fight."

He brushed a thumb across my hand in soft strokes — each slower and softer than the last.

"I've been watching you since that first encounter at Starbucks," he admitted, cheeks warming. "Not stalking — observing. Trying to figure out how to approach you without overwhelming you. You reminded me of where I came from… who I used to be… and who I still wanted to be."

I blinked, stunned.

"I'm just a customer service rep."

"You're the man who feeds the homeless," he countered. "Who paints. Who writes dreams in diaries. Who loves Disney and wants magic to be real. Who believes in loyalty and honesty when most people abandon those virtues?"

He squeezed my hand gently.

"You were never 'just' anything."

My throat tightened.

"Gabriel…"

He leaned in slowly, brushing my forehead with the softest kiss.

"You saved my life, Nathan. And now—I want to spend my life with you. Not someday. Not eventually. Now. And in every tomorrow."

I stared at him.

Heart hammering. Chest aching. Breath shaking.

"Are you…" My words tangled. "Are you asking me to be your—"

"Yes," he whispered. "Mine."

(38) Learning How to Breathe Again

The next forty-eight hours passed in a strange mixture of exhaustion, comfort, and a warmth I didn't expect to feel in a hospital bed. Pain meds dulled the worst of the stabbing sensations in my chest, but what truly held me together was the constant presence of one man.

Gabriel.

He stayed by my side like gravity itself. Not hovering, not suffocating — simply *there*, solid and steady and warm like an anchor set in the deepest part of the ocean.

Every time I blinked awake, he was holding my hand, straightening my blankets, texting Emerson for updates, or reading softly beside me.

Sometimes he didn't notice I was awake and I would just…Watch him.

His lashes lowered in thought. The faint shadow of stubble along his jaw. The way his fingers touched the bullet necklace when he worried. The care in every movement.

This was the man who'd been feared in corporate boardrooms, hunted by a madman, and hardened by loss — and now he was brushing the hair off my forehead like I was the only person left in the world.

"You're staring," he murmured without looking up.

"How'd you know?"

"You always stare the same way," he said softly. "Like you're memorizing me."

"Maybe I am."

He lifted his eyes, and God… those eyes.

Warm brown, flecked with gold, framed by grief and hope and relief all at once.

"Nathan…" His voice trembled. "You almost died. I'm still trying to process that."

"Then process this," I said, reaching weakly toward his hand. He caught mine instantly. "I lived. Because of you. Because I needed more time with you."

His breath hitched — the kind of sound a man makes when his heart cracks open wider.

Hailey burst into the room on the third morning like a firework.

"OH MY GOD, NATHAN!" she shouted, knocking a tray of pudding cups off the side table. "You're alive! I swear to God if you ever die again I'll kill you!"

"Medically impossible," I muttered.

"Shut up," she sniffed, hugging me gently around the shoulders. "You're stuck with me forever."

She rounded on Gabriel next.

"And YOU," she pointed at him accusingly, "better take care of this man. If you don't, I will find you, billionaire status or not, and I will throw hands."

Gabriel bowed his head slightly, amused.

"Understood," he said. "Completely."

"Good," she huffed, then brightened. "Love the room, by the way."

My parents visited shortly after. Dad hugged me — awkward but powerful. Mom kissed my forehead as she used to when I'd scrape my knees as a kid.

But it was their reaction to Gabriel that floored me.

Mom hugged him.

Hugged him.

Dad shook his hand with both of his.

"We owe you everything," Dad said quietly. "That's not a debt we take lightly."

Gabriel swallowed hard.

"You owe me nothing," he murmured. "Nathan… Nathan is the gift." "Well," Mom spoke up, "In Hebrew, 'Nathan' does translate as 'Gift of God'."

I flushed.

Gabriel was in deep thought. Mom radiated. Dad sniffed. Hailey rolled her eyes at the ceiling.

That evening, after the visitors left and the nurses dimmed the lights, the room filled with a soft hush. The kind that's only found in hospital hallways late at night when machines hum like lullabies.

Gabriel sat beside me, one leg tucked under him, the bullet pendant resting over his heart. He traced the curve of my knuckles with his thumb.

"You scared me more than anything ever has," he whispered.

"You know," I said, "this is the part where you're supposed to say I looked heroic."

He smiled faintly.

"You did. But I never want to see you look that heroic again."

"You know I can't promise that."

He leaned forward — slowly, checking my breathing, watching my chest — and pressed his lips to my forehead.

It wasn't a passionate kiss.

Not a desperate one.

It was a promise.

Steady. Sure. Undeniable.

"I love you," he said softly, the words slipping out so naturally he seemed surprised by them.

My heart fluttered like it had wings.

"I love you too," I whispered.

His eyes closed, and his shoulders sagged —

Relief. Release. And something like peace.

He climbed gently onto the side of the bed — careful not to jostle my wound — and laid beside me, our hands intertwined, our foreheads touching.

And for the first night since I'd nearly died, I breathed without pain.

Because he was there. Because we were whole again. Because the future no longer felt impossible.

Just beginning.

(39) The Dust Settles, The Future Clears

Hospitals are strange places when the crisis is over. Quiet, almost reverent. Like the building itself is catching its breath after holding so many others.

For the first time in days, the fear had faded. What remained was planning — debriefing — rebuilding.

And a future.

Our future.

Mr. Emerson arrived early the next morning, flanked by two analysts and one security partner I hadn't met before. He looked exhausted but collected, the kind of tired only brilliance earns.

"Nathan," he greeted me gently. "I'm relieved to see you upright."

"Upright is generous," I muttered. "Tilted diagonally, maybe."

He smiled politely, then got to business.

The way geniuses do.

"We've fully analyzed the remains of the remote detonator," Emerson said, placing a protective case on the table. "It was a modified Ying-Tao dual-trigger with a manual override — highly illegal, extremely unstable, and poorly handled by Calvin."

"Poorly handled seems like his brand," I said.

Gabriel squeezed my hand under the blanket.

Emerson continued.

"As for your family," Emerson continued, adjusting the papers in his hand, "there were no adverse effects after the grenades were removed the night of the incident. It was trauma-filled, yes — but Hailey and your parents were absolute troopers. The

244

disarm teams pulled it off within the thirty-second window without a single mistake."

Hailey wiped her nose, giving me a shaky smile. Dad squeezed Mom's shoulder. Gabriel exhaled a long breath of relief — the kind you let out only after knowing just how close you came to losing everything.

"Additionally," Emerson said, shifting papers, "we've traced Calvin's funding channels. Every fraudulent account, every shell company, every illegal offshore pipeline he used has been seized."

I blinked.

"Meaning?"

"Meaning," Emerson said with faint dry humor, "Calvin Marshall died both broke and stupid."

Hailey snorted. Dad muttered, "Good."

Gabriel said nothing — only looked at me with soft pride and relief.

"Now," Emerson continued, opening another file, "as for Gabriel's Sogno Toscano…"

Gabriel stiffened.

"My restaurant," he said quietly.

Emerson nodded. "The bomb planted in your private dining suite was traced back to Lopez's compromised phone. Calvin provided instructions. Lopez enabled access."

"Where is Lopez now?" Gabriel asked, voice cool as steel.

"In custody," Emerson replied. "Recovering from… his injuries."

Hailey whispered, "Nathan shot him in the nuts." My mom gasped. Dad stifled a laugh. Gabriel smirked, ever so slightly.

"As for the restaurant," Emerson resumed, "the explosion destroyed three internal rooms and the electrical grid. Fire suppression systems saved the main structure."

I swallowed. "And the settlement?"

Emerson's eyes glimmered.

"Well. That's where things get interesting."

He slid a form forward.

"The city insurance committee approved your claim. Gabriel's Sogno Toscano will receive full coverage: reconstruction, renovation, and business loss compensation."

"So, what's the catch?" Gabriel asked.

"No catch," Emerson said. "You're being granted a historic preservation extension."

"That sounds fancy," I whispered.

"It is," Emerson replied. "It allows Gabriel to rebuild with unlimited aesthetic freedom. He can redesign the entire restaurant — and the city will pay most of it."

I turned to Gabriel.

He stared at Emerson in disbelief.

"You mean—"

"Yes," Emerson said. "You can build it back better than ever. The entire establishment. Any style. Any theme. Any function."

Gabriel looked stunned.

Then he looked at me.

A spark of an idea was forming. A dream. A future.

Emerson's tone shifted back to business.

"Given the severity of the incident, Gabriel's protection team has increased its coverage. Two agents will always shadow Nathan until further notice. One embedded in your residence. One in your workplace. Additional surveillance for all immediate family and close associates."

"Meaning me?" Hailey asked, raising a brow.

"Yes," Emerson said.

"Meaning Bill too?" I asked.

"He's already got more security than the Pentagon," Emerson muttered. "He insisted on it."

That sounded like Bill.

By late afternoon, my discharge papers were signed. A hospital worker arrived with a wheelchair, but Gabriel lifted a brow.

"He's walking," he said gently but firmly.

"I am?" I blinked.

He smirked.

"With help."

And so — with careful support — Gabriel helped me stand, helped me dress, helped me breathe when the pain spiked. The nurse blushed. My mother filmed the whole thing. Hailey whispered under her breath, "Marry him already."

We made it to the elevator slowly, step by step, until I leaned against Gabriel's side, feeling him breathe out relief.

Outside, the late sun warmed the world.

A sleek armored vehicle waited at the curb.

"VIP transport," Gabriel murmured. "Just for today."

"Fancy," I teased.

He kissed my temple—soft, brief, and reverent.

"You're fancy," he whispered.

My chest fluttered.

When we arrived at my building — fully repaired, painted, and safe — I was expecting security guards, maybe Emerson waiting in the lobby, maybe some neighbors greeting me.

I was *not* expecting what I saw.

A banner hung across the hallway. It was totally hand-painted by Hailey.

It said:

WELCOME HOME NATHAN. STOP GETTING SHOT. LOVE, THE MANAGEMENT.

I laughed so hard my stitches hurt.

But the real surprise waited inside my apartment.

Gabriel opened the door slowly.

Lights flicked on.

And I froze.

My living room had been completely restored — better than before — with a new sofa, an upgraded entertainment system, fresh paint, a wardrobe reconstructed, a bathroom fully repaired, and on my table…A small box wrapped in deep blue ribbon.

"For you," Gabriel said quietly.

I opened it slowly.

Inside was a thin metal plate engraved with:

Nathan Moffett Survivor • Hero • Mine

I swallowed through a lump the size of a boulder.

"You didn't have to—"

"I did," he whispered.

His voice shook. Because he almost lost me. Because we almost lost everything.

He took my hand, lifting it gently.

"Your chapter with danger is ending," he said. "But your chapter with me is only beginning."

My breath caught.

"And soon," he added softly, "there will be another chapter… something bigger. Something extraordinary."

I blinked up at him.

"What chapter is that?"

He smiled — secretly, knowingly, lovingly.

"You'll see."

(40) Horizon Rising

Morning sunlight poured in warm and golden, draping over my blankets like a blessing. My chest still ached from the wound — a dull, persistent throb — but it was the kind of ache that let you know you survived something worth surviving.

For the first time in weeks, my apartment wasn't in shambles. For the first time in weeks, I wasn't alone. And for the first time in… maybe my whole damn life… the future didn't feel like a distant dream.

It felt possible and real.

Gabriel appeared in my doorway, barefoot, holding two mugs of steaming tea. He was wearing a fitted charcoal sweater, sleeves pushed up, hair tousled — the soft domestic version of a man who could order a tactical assault with the same hand that now held my mug.

He smiled when he saw I was awake.

"Good morning, sunshine."

I blinked. "This is illegal. No man should look this good at 8 a.m."

He chuckled, set a mug on my nightstand, and sat on the edge of the bed. "You slept through three security checks, an update call from Emerson, and a full breakfast delivery. I was beginning to worry."

"Well," I yawned, "getting shot takes a lot of beauty rest."

His face softened. He leaned down and kissed my forehead — slow and full of something I didn't dare name yet.

"We have things to discuss today," he said gently. "Good things."

He handed me an envelope. Simple. White. Classy.

Inside was a formal letter.

I recognized the corporate seal immediately.

My employer.

"What… what is this?" I asked.

Gabriel grinned. "Your new position."

I blinked down at the letter.

Community Engagement Ambassador. Monday–Friday. Weekends off permanently. Salary doubled. The office location moved to the building next door. Special travel opportunities.

"What—how—Gabriel, I didn't—"

"You earned it," he interrupted softly. "They saw what you did. How strong you were. How steady. How loyal. Mr. Emerson may have made a few pointed recommendations—" he coughed—"but you earned this title every step of the way."

My eyes warmed.

I felt… seen. Valued. Finally safe enough to breathe.

Later that afternoon, we stood in a small garden behind the community center, a peaceful place with flowers Marcus would have loved.

A framed picture of him rested on a table draped in blue.

Just a handful of us stood there — me, Hailey (arm around my shoulder), my parents, Gabriel, Bill (quiet for once), and Mr. Emerson.

The wind was soft. The sky was pale.

I stepped forward.

"Marcus wasn't the loudest," I began softly. "He wasn't the funniest. He wasn't the bravest. But he was one of the best friends I ever had."

My throat tightened. Gabriel moved closer behind me — just close enough for me to know he was there.

"He didn't go looking for danger. He didn't ask to be involved. He was pulled into darkness by someone who didn't know what light looked like. But Marcus still fought. He fought to survive. And he fought to warn us, even in agony. He saved us."

Hailey sniffed loudly.

"And now," I said, voice wavering, "it's our turn to honor him by living fuller, kinder, louder… and together."

I placed a single sunflower next to his photo.

Bright. Bold. Unshaken.

Bill muttered, "He'd like that."

Gabriel rested a hand on the small of my back.

We stood in silence as the wind carried the last moments of goodbye.

Gabriel leaned back against the foot of the bed, his hand linked gently with mine, our rings brushing together with a soft metallic whisper. The room was dim now, lit only by the low glow of the bedside lamp, casting warm honey shadows along the walls.

"You know something?" he asked quietly.

"What's that?" I murmured.

"I've been thinking a lot about… what happens next. After all this." His thumb traced over my palm in slow, grounding circles.

"Next?" I echoed. "Like, you and me next? Or… life, next?"

He smiled — that small, private smile he only gave when something mattered.

"Both."

I felt my pulse lift. He looked away briefly, searching the wall as it might steady him.

"There's… something I've been preparing for you," he said slowly, his voice careful, weighted with significance. "Something bigger than anything you and I have faced yet."

My brows lifted. "Preparing… how?"

Gabriel breathed in, chest rising deeply, then leaned closer. His forehead touched mine gently — a gesture like a promise.

"You once wrote," he whispered, "that some dreams feel too big to ever come true."

My breath hitched. He couldn't mean— He couldn't—

"And I want you to know," he continued softly, "I don't believe any dream of yours is too big. Or too impossible. You just needed the right person to help carry the magic."

I stared at him, unable to speak.

Gabriel smiled softly, thumb brushing my cheek. "Soon, Nathan. I'll show you soon. Something magical. Something you wished on a star for."

A tiny, stunned breath escaped me.

"You promise?" I whispered.

"I swear it," he said, sealing it with a kiss to my forehead. "A hint? One hint," I murmured, breath trembling with anticipation.

Gabriel leaned down, lips near my ear.

"It starts with a castle," he whispered.

My heart soared. A chill ran through me, electric and warm.

A castle. A wish. A dream I had buried so deep it felt like childhood.

He pulled back, eyes full of quiet excitement.

"Rest now," he murmured. "Tomorrow… we take the next step. Together."

I lay back, feeling the weight of his promise settle like golden light in my chest.

A castle. A dream. Magic on the horizon.
And Gabriel was all mine.

(41) EPILOGUE - "A Kingdom With My Name On It."

My apartment didn't look like a crime scene anymore. New floors, fresh paint, a custom wardrobe, restored furniture — Gabriel's teams had turned chaos into calm. A scented candle flickered near the window, the kind Hailey used to tease me about, and for the first time in weeks, the place felt like *mine* again.

I was standing — bruised, bandaged, sore, but upright — when the knock came.

Three soft taps.

The kind that one person seemed to use.

When I opened the door, Gabriel stood there in a fitted black coat, crisp shirt open at the collar, the necklace with the bullet I took for him glinting just above his chest. His hair was slightly windblown, his eyes warm and full of something that made my stomach flip.

"You ready?" he asked softly.

"For what?" I laughed nervously. "You look like you're about to take me to Narnia."

He smiled. "Close."

He offered his hand. I took it.

He led me out the door, down the elevator, and into a sleek black SUV waiting at the curb. The drive was quiet in a charged way — like something enormous was humming in the air between us.

Twenty minutes later, we pulled into a secured building I had never seen before — reflective glass, private entry, guards who bowed when Gabriel approached.

Inside, the elevator took us to the very top.

When the doors opened…

The room before us was breathtaking.

Floor-to-ceiling windows. A long maple table. And standing at the far end — a man in a navy suit with a Disney castle pin on his lapel.

Gabriel angled toward me. "That," he whispered, "is Christopher Valen. Vice Chairman of the Walt Disney Company."

My heart plummeted into my socks.

"Mr. Moffett," the Vice Chairman said warmly, stepping forward, "it is an honor to finally meet you."

"Meet me?" I squeaked.

He laughed gently. "Yes. We've been reviewing your file, your creative work, your background, your… rather impressive psychological resilience."

He motioned to the table behind him.

Laid out neatly were:

- A Disney-blue leather folder edged in gold
- A box tied with navy satin ribbon
- A castle-shaped brass keycard
- A gold pen engraved with *Enchantment*
- And a document in the center that stopped my heart.

Gabriel placed his hand at the small of my back and guided me closer.

Christopher continued, "Gabriel has spoken extensively about your vision. Your passion for storytelling. And your dream — the one you once wrote in a private diary. The dream you were too afraid to show the world."

My breath caught.

Gabriel's thumb brushed my spine.

The Vice Chairman opened the blue folder gently and handed it to me.

Inside, in elegant script:

The Enchantment Realms Initiative Appointment of Executive Leadership Chief Enchantment Realm Director & President Appointee: Nathan Leigh Moffett

I couldn't breathe.

Gabriel knelt — not proposing, not yet — but holding my free hand as if anchoring me to the earth.

"It was always meant for you," he whispered. "I've been building this with Disney for months. You once wished on a star… and I made it my mission to bring that wish back to you."

Christopher smiled softly and stepped aside.

"This division will be yours to lead," he said. "Creative development, immersive experiences, interactive fairytale live events, elite-level storytelling—everything we're preparing for the next evolution of the parks. You'll have full access across all

Disney resorts, lifetime privileges, and a dedicated office at Magic Kingdom.”

He paused, letting gravity sink in.

“And when the time comes… the castle is yours.”

My knees nearly gave.

“And,” Gabriel added quietly, reaching behind him, “there’s one more thing.”

He opened the small white box with the navy ribbon.

Inside were two rings:

Mine — platinum with star-constellation engraving and an inscription that read: “For the man who jumped.” His — black titanium edged in platinum with a single sapphire.

He took a breath that trembled slightly.

“Nathan… I’m not asking you to marry me today.” He smiled, tender and full of promise. “I’m asking you to begin our future with these two promise rings.”

I lifted my hand slowly. He lifted the ring and slid the platinum ring onto my finger. It fit perfectly, like destiny carved its size. With his, my trembling fingers guided the second ring onto his ring finger.

“A pre-engagement promise ring,” he murmured. “A vow that we’re choosing each other. That’s what we’re building now… is forever. So, no rush for marriage. No pressure”

I swallowed hard, tears stinging hot at the corners of my eyes.

“And when we’re ready,” he whispered against my cheek, “I’ll give you the proposal you always dreamed of. In front of the castle you’ve loved since childhood. ONE DAY.”

My voice shook:

“This… this is real?”

Gabriel kissed my forehead, slow and warm.

"This is real," he said. "This is us."

I closed my eyes, the future unfolding like fireworks inside me.

A castle. A kingdom. A life. A love that survived flames, bullets, betrayal, and chaos.

I smiled through my tears.

"This must be what magic feels like," I whispered.

Gabriel held me tighter.

"No," he murmured softly.

"This is what *forever* feels like."

BOOK ONE — OUTRO "Where Dreams Turn Toward Tomorrow"

Every story has a moment where the storm breaks. Where danger loosens its grip. Where wounds begin to heal, and the heart makes room for possibility.

For Nathan, the battles had been fierce:

- A deranged enemy from Gabriel's past
- Explosives, threats, riddles, and bloodshed
- A friend lost, and innocence shattered
- A life overturned by shadows and secrets

But in the ashes of chaos, something stronger emerged— A love forged under pressure. A partnership tested in fire. A truth more powerful than the danger surrounding them.

Nathan survived. Gabriel endured. Together, they found a path back to light.

Now, with a ring on Nathan's finger and a kingdom waiting beyond the horizon…one chapter closes. Another hums alive.

Magic is no longer a distant wish. It is a promise. A future. A doorway.

And as Nathan steps into tomorrow—hand in hand with the man who risked everything to meet him under the castle of his heart— A new kind of story begins.

One where love is the adventure. Where dreams are blueprints. Where kingdoms aren't inherited… but built.

Book One closes here. But the star Nathan once wished upon is only just beginning to shine.